# The Seer's Womb

## A Novel

Jessica Johnson

DozierRose Books 🌹

## Content Warning

This novel explores sensitive and potentially triggering themes, including explicit sexual content, sexual violence, rape, emotional and physical abuse, infertility trauma, and dark supernatural elements. The dark supernatural nature of this book may be distressing for some readers. Please read with care. Your well-being matters.

The Seer's Womb

A Novel

Published by DozierRose Books, Texas, USA.

Imprint Logo: DozierRose Books ❦

ISBN (Paperback): 979-8-9939336-0-3

Cover design by Jessica Johnson

Interior design by DozierRose Books

Printed in the United States of America.


First Edition

DozierRose Books ❦

*Dedication*

*For every woman who has ever created, nurtured, or*
*endured—*
*You are the beginning of every story.*

*In ancient folklore, storks are said to carry more than good
luck and fertility—*
*They carry the souls waiting to be born.*
*The stork is more than a bearer of life—*
*It is the soul's messenger, crossing between womb and sea.*
*Those it carries are never truly new,*
*only returning from where the tide last took them.*

Table of Contents

# Prologue

Rovona, the forgotten village by the water, nestled on a rocky coastline where the olive orchards meet the cliffs. Crouched on the cliffs like a secret; built of pale stone and faded terracotta. Children darted barefoot between the crooked buildings, daring one another to touch the cliff's edge, while old women rocked on porches, knitting and telling tales of tricksters and spirits beneath the waters. The village of Rovona had survived centuries by stubborn magic, by charm and curse alike, and it seemed to watch over those born within its walls with a secretive, knowing patience.

Long ago, a blind child wandered into the sea one moonless night. Salt waves stung her skin, but she did not turn back. The small child's eyes lifted to the dark water, and a whispered plea passed between the child and the tide.

"Give me sight."

"Not mere vision, but powerful sight. I want to see what no other can."

Even though the small child's voice was soft and gentle, it carried something more—like the tide's hush before a storm.

The sea spirits stirred. Their voices curling over the waves like froth, sly and mischievous.

"We shall give you sight."

"You shall see threads of fate, the turning of time, and secrets buried deeper than the tide itself. But you will not see without cost.

"'Anything." The small child whispered into the sea.

The water laughed around her, cold and endless, playful and cruel. The child stumbled back to shore, eyes burning with unearthly fire. She could see everything, the hidden currents of the world, the secret stirrings of hearts but the bargain itself, she remembered nothing.

The elders of Rovona knew the sea spirits were tricksters. They had whispered warnings through generations, teaching caution in every glance at the waves, in every footstep near the cliff's edge. Yet even they could not prevent what had been done, nor could they undo the bargain that lay hidden beath the tides.

# Chapter 1: The Sea's Pact

Centuries ago, born by the Mediterranean Sea, Colette remembered running barefoot through the olive orchards as a child. The air was heavy with sweetness when the sun burned hottest, her favorite time of year. She would pick figs and smear their juices across her lips, chase lizards through crumbling stone walls, and fall asleep outdoors listening to the sea whisper its melodies against the rocks.

Growing up in the small village of Rovona, Colette was the only child with fiery orange hair, which her mother insisted she hide beneath patterned scarves. The other children accepted her playful spirit, yet her essence unsettled them some. They watched her with wary eyes, for she often stared too long at the waves or spoke of things she could not possibly know. Over time, their affection for her mingled with unease, and their careless words hardened her.

As a young woman, she still keeps her curls hidden and at night she often awoke with her heart racing, haunted by a recurring dream of childhood. In it, the olive trees rustled, the sea hissed, and the children of Rovona circled her, pointing and calling her witch. A dark-haired boy with a long nose began the chant, and soon the others joined. The dream never changed; the dirt-stained faces, the dull-colored clothes, the cruel harmony of their voices. Most eight-year-old girls would have run home in tears, but not Colette. She stood in the circle smiling. Pulling the scarf from her head, she let her curls bounce free and challenged their chant with a riddle:

*"Cry, cry, you will die.*
*Die, die, you will cry.*
*Break your tooth and burn your eye.*
*Break the wings and still you fly."*

The words spilled from her without thought. Louder and louder, she spoke, until her voice overpowered theirs. Frightened, the children scattered.

That is always the moment she wakes up. Frustrated, wishing her dreams held potential lovers instead of old cruelties. Her mother had called those odd phrases "silly riddles," they had followed Colette through childhood, escaping her in moments of fear, joy, or shame. Through the years, Colette's words flowed like the sea itself, shifting, curling, and breaking in unpredictable ways. Questions became riddles, answers twisted upon themselves, and even the simplest statements carried hidden currents. Years passed, and the children who once mocked her grew into superstitious adults, filled with guilt. In time they grew protective, whispering that she guarded the village in ways they could not explain.

Colette truly enjoyed wandering Rovona's market, not to buy, but to watch. She loved observing people's gestures, mannerisms, laughter, even the sadness in their eyes. Sometimes she followed the same person for hours, creating an imagined bond without ever speaking a word.

Her presence was hard to miss. She walked with confidence, hips swaying, coins clinking on the scarf at her waist. Once mocked and chased, she now moved through Rovona as though it belonged to her. Even with her orange curls hidden, her beauty could not be concealed. Her skin was pale, her cheeks often rose colored from too much sun, her eyes dark and flirtatious. She thrived on catching the gaze of strangers, then turning to see if they were still watching her.

At night, she teased drunkards at the local tavern, danced with the musicians, and made coins from her movements. She never drank, keeping her mind sharp against danger, though she had many protectors in the room. Rarely did she need them, her wit and charm could dissolve most threats.

She was known as the woman who reads palms, her soft fingers tracing unseen lines while her words uncovered hidden fears and unspoken desires. Even amongst the tavern's chaos, she could make someone feel safe and vulnerable. Often people confided secrets she never asked for. When the music played, she danced as if neither no one nor everyone were watching. The fiddle and drum always pulling her to the center of the room, like a tide.

The locals knew her well, if she wasn't dancing or telling fortunes, she was with a man.

Colette craved the company of men, the heat of desire, the taste of a good kisser and the grip of strong hands wanting her. In her moments of passion, she always let down her hair; not at first though, as she enjoyed the teasing, the biting, the mystery of someone's body. She never let down her hair until they were already inside her. When her hair fell, it was like orange vines of ivy that could wrap around the other person and press them deeper.

Deeper into her bliss.

Some men swore her eyes glowed like embers in the dark, burning brighter with the strength of her lover.

Through the years, she discovered her eye contact was a true weapon. No need to have a sharp blade if you have someone in hypnosis with a mere look. The people of Rovona learned to be careful when approaching her, for her mood fluctuated as rain does. Shifting like the sea; some days playful and radiant, spreading joy through the village; other days, crushed beneath grief so heavy she forgot how to breathe; and sometimes, consumed by a fever of rage and lust that left others powerless under her spell.

But Colette's passion held a purpose.

Pleasure was never just pleasure. Every whispered kiss, every night in a lover's arms brought her closer to a single desire:

She wanted a baby more than anything. To bear a child of her own.

To her, motherhood was more than life, it was legacy. She wanted more than touch, more than fleeting praise, more than the ache of being desired. She yearned to create, truly yearned to shape life from her own body, to cradle a child that was hers alone, a child who would silence mockery and tie her firmly to the earth.

The locals often whispered that she had made a pact with the sea spirits, trading her womb for the gift of sight. In their tellings, the curse was not only barrenness, but a hunger for a child that would haunt her through every tide. They claimed the ocean marked her, that each wave carried her sorrow, and that the wind itself carried her longing back to shore. Some feared her, believing the sea still owned her. Others pitied her, saying no mortal heart could bear such a bargain without breaking.

But she would not be broken.

No matter the cost, she would keep trying for a child, and nothing, neither fate nor spirits, would stand in her way.

## Chapter 2: Nest

Colette lost her mother before she learned what death truly meant; a couple years after her first bleed. She never knew the true reason for her mother's death but even at her young age, she knew the sea had something to do with it.

Everything in Rovona led back to the sea.

For a year or so afterward, she stopped speaking much. The villagers said she'd gone quiet out of sorrow, but it was more than that. Words felt too small for what swelled inside her. When she spoke, her voice came out soft and uneven, like someone else was borrowing it.

Through her youth, her emotions came in tides; high, consuming, and unpredictable. Some days she laughed too hard at nothing; other days she'd burst into tears without knowing why. Without a mother's hand to guide her, Colette didn't know how to hold herself together. There was no one to teach her that sensitivity could be strength, or that sight and feeling might be the same thing. When storms rolled over Rovona, she felt them inside her chest. She also became aware, when others were angry, she carried their anger too.

That first year after her mother's death, she often took to walking the cliffs alone at dusk, following the rhythm of the waves because it reminded her of her mother's breathing when she slept. There, she could cry without reason and not feel foolish. The sea, at least, understood that emotions didn't always need explanations.

One evening, the sky turned the color of bruised peaches, heavy with the scent of salt and rain. Colette followed a trail of broken shells down to the lower ridge, her feet bare and dusty. That's when she saw it—

a stork tangled in a fishing net, one long leg pinned beneath the reeds. It struggled weakly, its white feathers streaked with mud. She knelt beside it, heart pounding.

"Shh," she whispered, though her hands trembled. "I'll help you."

The bird stilled. Its dark eye met hers, calm and ancient, as if it already knew her. Carefully, she worked the net loose, pulling strand by strand until the last knot gave way. When she touched its wing, something rushed through her—a warmth that wasn't hers. For a breathless moment, she saw her mother standing in the window, the scent of rosemary thick in the air, her hands washing Colette's hair. The memory was so clear it hurt.

Then it was gone.

The stork rose, shook the water from its feathers, and took flight. As it lifted into the wind, a strip of cloth from the net—red, frayed—fluttered free and landed in Colette's lap. The same shade as her mother's shawl. She sat there long after the bird disappeared, the cloth clutched in her hand. Her chest ached, but not from sadness.

It was something else; something fierce and new.

That night, she dreamed of a nest made of salt grass and seaweed, with a woman's voice humming above it. When she woke, she realized her mother wasn't truly gone, only carried somewhere she couldn't reach. And for the first time, Colette felt the longing to carry life of her own and how powerful It would be to build her own nest.

From then on, the villagers noticed her watching the storks that nested on the rooftops. Sometimes she would climb to the roof to have a closer look and watch the storks repair their nests; one bringing twigs, the other pressing them into place, patient and sure. Their movements steadied her. Each spring they returned to what they'd built, mending the same structure again and again.

Colette understood them. She, too, wanted to build something that could hold warmth through every season. She wanted to make a place where love stayed.

One day, when she was grown, she would.

Her nest would not hang from a roof or sway in a tree.

It would live inside her—beating, sheltering, giving.


Years later, when her sight began to show her things no one else could see; births, deaths, the faces of the lost—Colette often thought of that first stork.

Of the way it had looked at her, unafraid, as if recognizing one of its own.

# Chapter 3: Chaos to Case Notes

*Present Day*

Janell kept repeating the words in her head:
*Take three lives and replace them with three…*
*But know this,*
*in which lifetime could it be?*
*Grow three, but not from your family tree,*
*When this happens, you will clearly see…*

What is this, a riddle? A poem? She couldn't be sure. The phrases came to her in fragments at first, random thoughts and broken phrases scattered throughout her day and now they haunted her morning. Lately, her dreams faded before she could remember them, leaving only these cryptic words. She figured maybe a Netflix series had lodged itself in her subconscious.

She groaned, swatting her alarm. Why was she lying here, obsessing over riddles? She had already hit snooze twice.

Mondays were the worst. Coffee was non-negotiable.

Janell shuffled to the kitchen. She bought a new Amaretto-flavored creamer, and just that thought motivated her sleepy ass out of bed. Her hair didn't stand a chance of looking nice today—high bun it was.

Morning rituals began with coffee. The gurgling machine and the scent of brewed beans were familiar comforts. She pressed play on Pandora, tuning to the French station. She didn't speak French, aside from a few words—bonjour, merci—but she adored the music; sometimes soft, sometimes vibrant, always wrapping around her foggy mind and gently pulling her into the day. She sipped her coffee while doing the bare minimum of makeup. Janell juggled lunchboxes, backpacks and mismatched socks as the clock ticked mercilessly towards eight.

"Hurry up!" She called, her voice sharp but tired. Her youngest in a mood again about having to go to school at all. Cereal bowls sat half-eaten on the table, homework sprawled across the counter, and the dog barked at the chaos. With a sigh, she grabbed jackets and bag, her arms full but determination stronger. One by one, she nudged her three sleepy children toward the door, their dawdling tested her patience, but she pressed on, as she did every morning.

The drive to work was predictably frustrating. Traffic. Always traffic.

Janell parked in the familiar lot and switched on her "social worker brain." She was a wife, a mother, and a full-time social worker. Many assumed that meant taking children away; it didn't. She worked with the elderly. In nursing homes, there was usually only one social worker for the whole building. The social worker oversaw both the long-term and short-term rehabilitation side and acted as case manager for every resident. Morning meetings were routine. The administrator huddled with department managers to discuss admissions, discharges, hospital updates, conference call reminders, care plan times, staffing shortages, and nursing updates.

This was her fourth nursing home. The building was old, desperately needing an update, especially the front lobby furniture. When she'd interviewed, she didn't plan to stay long; she just needed something stable after moving. Eight months had passed, and the nine-to-five grind had a way of swallowing time.

The staff was predictable, a regional nurse acting as Director of Nursing, a permanently irritated business office manager, a couple of nursing managers who stuck together, an easy-going activity director, and the medical records manager who was always smiling and gossiping. The Administrator hid in her office, taking urgent calls and so-called meetings, but really avoiding the chaos of the day.

All the minor crises, they went to Janell.

Short-term rehab patients, she was their discharge planner. New resident issues, she handled them. Complaints: they always found her desk.

A resident is crying, anger, or frustrated; the social worker can help with that.

Everything funneled to her. She did everything.

Today's to-do list: four rehab residents going home this weekend, two needing wheelchairs, one possibly requiring portable oxygen. Doctor signatures were needed, but the doctor wouldn't be back this week. Home health referrals had to be set up; the fax machine was down. Two new admissions arrived yesterday, waiting for 48-hour care plan meetings. Therapy schedules conflicted with nursing and dietary. Janell was always expected to orchestrate the chaos herself.

A resident complaining about her roommate; another upset the dentist hadn't visited recently. In reference to the Dentist, she attempted to explain Medicaid approval delays, only to be called a liar. Nurses stopped her with more issues: male residents needing to move to a different hall, who is now refusing to shower, and complaints about staffing ratios. Her office was flooded with voicemails, emails, and hospice marketers at the door. In the living area, a resident fell while attempting to stand from her wheelchair; another was caught smoking outside again.

It was chaos, nonstop.

Being a social worker was hard to explain, especially when people asked, "What is it that you do?"

"Well… everything," she wanted to say.

I do fucking everything. That should be the answer, she thought, though she rarely said it aloud.

Janell knew what it sounded like, and she knew what people were thinking: Why the hell does someone choose to be a social worker?

She couldn't speak to all social workers. She'd never worked with state agencies, never done school social work, never been at non-profits, so she didn't know what their days were like—maybe they were less stressful, maybe not.

You want the social worker answer?

"It's the small moments that make the stress worth it."

Umm… maybe. Kind of. Okay, not really. Hell, she didn't even know why she did it. But over time, she'd gotten pretty good at orchestrating the chaos inside the nursing home.

Okay, a small moment, for example. She had answered a call light the other day and walked into a resident's room. The resident couldn't reach her remote and asked for another blanket. When Janell placed it on the bed, the woman put her hand on hers and said, "Thank you."

"You're welcome," Janell replied naturally.

"No, thank you for everything. I see everything you do for everyone. You're always smiling and so helpful. This place wouldn't be the same without you."

Her hand was warm, fragile.

Janell wanted to cry at that moment. She needed to hear that appreciation. It felt so good, so necessary. She held the woman's hand, smiled, and thanked her for the kind words. In that instant, she realized the resident needed connection just as much as she did.

Two weeks later, that resident died.
Janell couldn't even remember her name.

By the way, if you work long enough in a nursing home, you became numb to death after a while.

Chapter 4: Creation's Call

Motherhood was a kind of power few could understand. Janell admired it; the way a woman's body could grow another life, nurture it, and bring it into the world. It was relentless, a strength unmatched. And she knew how to honor that power in herself and in others, recognizing the magic of creation wherever it appeared. After all, women were the keepers of life itself, and to witness that was nothing short of sacred.

On a very regular Saturday morning, Janell found herself at her favorite grocery store, H.E.B., observing the woman in front of her. It was early, around 8 a.m., the perfect time to shop before the Saturday rush. Blue Bell vanilla bean ice cream sat in the other woman's cart, a telltale sign of late-night cravings.

During a brief conversation, Janell learned the woman was 25 weeks pregnant with her second child. She couldn't help but admire her radiance, her long, healthy hair, the way her body carried life. She considered asking what prenatal supplements the woman took but restrained herself. Pregnancy, Janell believed, was enchanting and she didn't want to make anyone uncomfortable by staring too long.

Still, she was captivated. The woman wasn't just standing there; she was creating life. Her body was forming vital organs, a heart learning to beat, bones emerging from nothing. Magic was at work inside her. To be pregnant was to hold creation itself. This woman in the grocery store, this stranger; she was not just a mother—she was a maker of worlds.

As the woman thanked the cashier and moved toward the exit, she glanced at Janell with a small smile and a nod, cupping her growing belly. Without thinking, Janell cupped her own lower abdomen. She longed to be pregnant again.

Janell was a mother, but she was also a former surrogate. It was Janell's belief that a surrogate, was pure power—a real-life goddess who grew a miracle for someone else. She had carried for two families and was beginning her third and final surrogacy journey soon. She had children of her own and didn't necessarily want more, but she adored being pregnant.

Surrogacy was a process. Janell had created a detailed profile of herself; discussing her work, home environment, marital status, children, support system, and medical history. Every previous medical detail and/or complication had to be disclosed. Most importantly, she explained why she wanted to be a gestational surrogate. Surrogates, she often reminded herself, didn't use their own eggs—they were "just the oven."

Her curiosity had begun with a friend who couldn't carry children. Watching Janell navigate three complication-free pregnancies sparked questions and fascination. IVF had been too expensive for her friend, but the process from the surrogate's perspective intrigued Janell. With her friend's encouragement, she explored the process and found herself enthralled. She wanted to be with child again.

Pregnancy always made Janell feel... powerful.

Strange, she knew, but true. Many women focused on the negatives: morning sickness, fatigue, mood swings, aches, stretch marks. Janell felt them too, but they were always outweighed by euphoria. Pregnancy, she believed, was a form of supernatural power.

She had once read that a goddess was a conscious woman of power. And what could be more powerful than creating life? Populating the Earth. Even the question of when a soul enters the body fascinated her, though opinions varied by religion and philosophy. Janell knew she was meant to be pregnant again.

It was a calling, a purpose.

Somewhere, a family needed her. Somewhere, someone was weeping, fearing it would never happen for them. Someone feared they would never know the love of parenthood.

Surrogacy gave them hope.

Janell's awareness was unmatched. She knew she could help.

Her body could help.

Her mental strength was exceptional. Her womb was powerful. Her desire to aid others was deeply rooted.

Maybe… just maybe… that was why she made such a great surrogate.

# Chapter 5: Guiding Light

The first light always found Rovona before it found the rest of the coast. The village sat like a bowl cupped by cliffs, cradling its people close. When the sun rose, the mist lifted from the rooftops, revealing a scatter of blue shutters, whitewashed walls, and clay pots bursting with rosemary and thyme.

From her window, Colette could hear the rhythm of the morning—the crack of bread loaves being split, the shouts of fishermen greeting the day, the laughter of women hanging laundry strung between houses. The sea carried their voices, softening them into something that almost sounded like song.

Rovona was not grand, but it was alive. Its people worked hard, loved fiercely, and believed in small magics. A pinch of salt behind the door. A seashell placed on the windowsill to keep the storms away. Coins left at the old shrine not out of fear, but gratitude—for a calm sea, a safe return, a child's laughter.

Colette did love the market the most. The air thick with the smell of figs, lemons, and olive oil. The fish glimmering like shards of moonlight on ice. The women calling each other "sister" even when they weren't, their words quick and teasing. Here, no one hurried. Life moved at the pace of tides and stories.

Colette sometimes felt like a ghost walking among them, someone set apart by what she saw and what she couldn't explain. When she walked through the square, people nodded, respectful and knowing, as if they sensed that her connection to the sea was not a curse, but a calling. At dusk, the whole village seemed to exhale. The air turned honey-colored, and laughter spilled from doorways. Families gathered for evening meals, candles flickering through window glass. To Colette, Rovona was more than a place; it was a heartbeat, ancient, imperfect, but faithful. Steady in its own rhythm, carrying the lives of its people like waves carrying shells, never questioning where they'd come from, only returning them home again.

That evening, the tavern pulsed with noise, laughter, and the sour-sweet scent of ale. Men shouted over one another, tankards clashed, and the fiddle kept the room spinning. Colette let her body move to the rhythm; her lips curled in a smile that answered the room's hunger for joy.

But in the corner, away from the firelight, sat an old man. His hands trembled around a half-empty cup, his eyes drifting as though they had lost their anchor. While the others lived loudly, he seemed to be slipping quietly into a place of his own.

Colette's chest ached at the sight. She had always felt a pull toward the elderly, as if the thinning threads of their days called out to her. To her, they were not shadows to be ignored but souls who carried entire worlds in their silence. She could never turn away from them.

She stepped away from the dancing and moved to his table. She offered him the simple gift of presence, a kind word, a gentle question, the warmth of someone who saw him when no one else bothered to look. His eyes softened, the fog lifting if only for a moment.

The tavern roared around them, wild and unrelenting, but for that brief time, there were only the two of them; one fading, the other refusing to let him disappear unseen.

Colette leaned closer, her voice gentle, "Let me walk you home," she offered.

The old man blinked, his gaze heavy with fatigue. For a moment he seemed uncertain, as if the words did not quite reach him. Confusion clouded his face, but beneath it was a quiet relief, the way a child softens when someone takes their hand.

He gave a small nod.

"Aye… home," he murmured, though it sounded more like a question than an answer.

She smiled, steady and kind, rising from the bench to help him to his feet. His body leaned against hers, frail but trusting, and she guided him past the roaring laughter and clattering mugs.

The night air was cooler than the tavern's heavy warmth, carrying the salt of the sea and the faint smoke of hearth fires.

Colette steadied the old man as they stepped onto the cobblestones, his arm looped around hers, his steps slow and uncertain.

The village had quieted. Lantern lights painted soft halos along the narrow street, guiding their path. The old man muttered now and then, fragments of memory spilling like loose threads; a woman's name, the harvest long past, a boyhood story he could not finish.

Colette listened, nodding, offering the kind of silence that steadied rather than judged. She had no need to correct his wandering mind; it was enough that someone walked beside him, keeping him tethered to the world for a little while longer.

When they reached his crooked doorway, he looked at her as though surprised to already be home. His tired eyes filled with something softer than confusion, gratitude, perhaps, though no words came.

She pressed his hand gently before letting go.

"Rest well," she whispered, and watched as he shuffled inside.

Her lips curved into a faint smile. Guiding the old man had quieted something inside her, but the night was not yet finished. Pleasure and mischief still waited in the warm, smoky glow she had left behind. With a swish of her skirt, she turned and walked back toward the noise, ready to be swept into it once more.

# Chapter 6: The Fortune Interrupted

The tavern's warmth and smoke wrapped around the night like a familiar cloak when a stranger stepped through the door, carrying the scent of the sea and far-off roads. Colette's gaze caught him immediately, he was tall, easy in his movements, with eyes that flickered curiosity and mischief in equal measure.

He scanned the room, and when his eyes landed on her, he lingered longer than etiquette demanded. There was a spark in that look, something teasing and unspoken, and Colette couldn't help but return it.

Luc lingered at the edge of the tavern, curiosity warring with caution. He had never believed in palm reading, had never even entertained the idea and yet something about her pulled at him, an invisible thread that made his chest tighten. He shifted his weight, half-smile faltering.

Colette stepped closer, her eyes warm but filled with quiet command. Before he could protest, she reached out and took his hand in hers. The moment their fingers touched, a shiver ran through him, subtle but undeniable, and all his resistance melted away. His breath caught, and he surrendered — not to magic, not entirely, but to the certainty that whatever she saw, he wanted to know.

Colette's fingers traced the lines of Luc's palm with practiced ease, her touch light yet intimate. She closed her eyes for a moment, letting the rhythm of his pulse and the shapes in his hand speak to her. A vision blossomed before her, it was bright, chaotic, and full of life. She saw a man who would father many children, whose laughter and presence would leave an imprint on countless lives. Her chest tightened with a warmth she hadn't expected; her fingers lingered a second longer, and she bit her bottom lip, a subtle, involuntary gesture. The thought stirred something deep inside her, something hungry and alive.

When she opened her eyes, Luc looked at her differently. The hesitant curiosity had shifted into fascination, and now, somehow, he seemed even more compelling; the very air around him charged, the allure of destiny wrapped around him like a cloak. Colette's heart skipped, and a slow, thrilling awareness settled over her, she was more than excited, and the night had only just begun.

Luc's hand still rested lightly in hers; Colette couldn't resist letting her fingers curl around his just enough to draw him closer. His hesitation had vanished; the spark in his eyes now mirrored her own.

"You've never had your fortune read before, have you?" she teased, tilting her head, her voice low and intimate, brushing against him like a whispered promise.

"Never," he admitted, voice thick with something he couldn't name. "And I... I don't know why I let you."

Her lips curved into a slow, knowing smile.

"Sometimes," she murmured, leaning closer,

"it's better to surrender."

Luc shivered under her touch, his gaze darkening with fascination and desire. He leaned in slightly, drawn by the magnetic pull of her presence, and she felt it, the tension between them, coiled tight, each glance and brush of fingers amplifying it.

Then the tavern erupted in sudden uproar.

A chair toppled with a crash, a shout split the air, and ale spilled across the floor. A fight had ignited near the doorway, fists swinging, voices rising, the room erupting into confusion.

Luc was swept into the brawl, his tall frame vanishing into the crush of bodies. Colette's fingers still tingling from his warmth, heart pounding with frustration and longing. She lingered by the doorway, arms crossed, lips pursed. That vision still pulsed in her mind; him, surrounded by children not yet born. She had been so certain he would be lying across her bed before dawn, his weight pressing her into the sheets, her desire answered.

Instead, the night had turned.

With no pleasure waiting, she exhaled slowly and decided she might as well head home.

# Chapter 7: Always Mine

In the early hours of the day, Colette could often be found sitting on her favorite rock by her favorite tree. When the wind picked up, she would close her eyes and let it embrace her skin. She loved being outside. Some days, she wandered barefoot through the fields behind her home, picking berries and mumbling her own type of poetry under her breath. There was a perplexing beauty to her; her mind seemed always elsewhere, yet her body moved with an effortless grace. Her words never followed a predictable path, and yet she would grin to herself and continue her whispered conversations, shining in her own private delight. Watching her was like watching art; the way her body swayed to music only she could hear. Many believed she carried an aura, a positive energy that could lift the spirits of the dullest of faces.

Today was market day.

She needed bread, jam, and seeds for the birds. She often left seeds on her cottage window seals for the birds to enjoy. She tied her orange curls back tightly, covering them with a silk maroon-and-taupe scarf, and grabbed her oversized basket. The market was just stirring to life, the scent of fresh-cut flowers filling the morning air.

"Good morning, Margot!" Colette called out. Margot was arranging bundles of lavender and motioned for her to come closer.

"Did you see him yet?" Margot asked, her eyes wide with excitement. "Jacques."

Colette's gaze swept through the crowd. She and Jacques had known each other for years. In their younger years, he had always been there when she needed someone to keep her company, or to watch her get into trouble. She knew he had once wanted more than friendship, though her attention had always shifted unpredictably. He had always been tall, skinny, and awkwardly handsome, but with a kind heart that matched Colette's mischievous nature.

Her eyes caught a woman she didn't recognize, standing behind a tall man. As he turned fully, Colette knew immediately— it was Jacques. He looked stronger, heavier, his face partially hidden by a scruffy beard. He kissed the woman on the forehead, speaking words that made her laugh.

Without thinking, Colette moved toward them, locking eyes with Jacques as she walked. His smile was slight, as if he tried to hide it, but it couldn't be controlled.

"Jacques! I cannot believe it—is that really you?" she called over the market chatter. She wrapped her arms around him, breaking his wife's hold. His eyes remained on her, trance-like, the fire between them unmistakable.

"It's been so many years. How have you been? I heard you moved back, is it true?" Colette asked.

"Yes, I'm back," he admitted.

"We… we moved back just two days ago," he added, stumbling slightly.

Up close, his wife was plain, very plain. Nothing too terrible, just unremarkable. Colette's gaze immediately returned to Jacques.

Her body burned with heat at the sight of him, the old hunger roaring back. The jealousy was instant as he touched the woman's shoulder, introducing her.

"This is Berenice, my wife," he said.

Berenice spoke softly but sharp, "Jacques has mentioned you several times Colette, but left out how beautiful you were."

Colette smirked inwardly. So plain, she thought.

She continued to admire Jacques, biting her lip at how much he had changed. Their eyes met again, magnetic and impossible to look away from.

A man's voice broke through the tension; "Fresh fish!"

Jacques motioned for Berenice to gather more vegetables, and she left. Colette whispered to herself, "Your wife is so sweet… so plain."

Jacques leaned in, whispering, "Meet me at the tavern later tonight. Please."

Colette considered for a moment, then smiled and nodded. She loved making men beg just a little. Turning to walk away, she let the breeze carry her scent. Jacques inhaled deeply, intoxicated, closing his eyes and biting his bottom lip. He then watched her walk back through the crowd. On her way back home, she giggled and swayed as she walked the dirt path; whispering words underneath her breath.

*"I know you're still mine…*
*even after so many moons.*
*I will moan your name later…*
*so deep inside; your wife will even swoon."*

Later that night in the tavern, Jacques waited for hours, watching the front door like a hawk. His ale cup was filled several times as he impatiently waited, biting his nails, twitching and anxious for Colette's arrival. Jacques swore his mind was playing tricks on him, as Colette's scent still tinkered in his nostrils from earlier in the day. He started to pace the room, pining for her, like a drug he desperately needed. When she finally walked into the tavern, his nerves settled; and for him it then felt like the moment the sun rises at dawn. Jacques walked over to her swiftly.

"Do you need a drink?" he asked.

Colette pressed her finger to her lips and told him to hush.

"Follow me," she spoke softly as if she was telling him a secret. Before Jacques could finish the rest of the ale in his cup and blink twice, Colette was walking towards the forest behind the tavern. She would look back at him, making sure he wasn't far behind. She carried this bewitching spirit all the time; making men do as she wanted, when she wanted it. Jacques was no stranger to this bewitching spirit; she always carried it, even when they were younger.

It was late, the forest was dark due to the tall trees hovering over them; but just enough moonlight piercing through the branches to make her look even more glimmering than she already was. He caught up to her, and attempted to kiss her but she pulled back, toying with him, not letting his lips meet hers.

She looked deeply in his eyes again, a hypnotic trance that was both frightening and arousing.

She untied the front part of his trousers, never breaking eye contact and nudged him back onto a grassy knoll.

When Colette wanted something, she often took it right away. She grasped Jacques' dick, as if it belonged to her, making sure it was alive and hard. She then pulled her skirt up and straddled his lap. She started teasing him with her pussy, letting the tip enter her just a little,

then not at all…

just a little, then not at all…

Over and over, she tortured him with mere moments of pleasure, then gladly took it away.

An enchantress of sex, she grew more aroused every time his face grimaced in pain when she pulled her wet slit away from him. Jacques couldn't take it anymore; he pressed himself all the way in; grabbing a hold onto her hips, so she couldn't retreat this time. He went deep and strong inside of her; her wetness was nothing short of magic.

Colette moaned and let down her curls.

"I've missed you," she moaned into his ear.

Her orange curls glowed in the moonlight as they bounced around her face and shoulders. She rocked her hips back and forth and leaned next to his ear as she moaned his name,

Jacques…

Jacques…

Jacques" …

Her moans became breath-eyer as she said his name more quickly, bouncing harder.

To slow things down, she finally kissed him.

Kissing turned into her sucking on his bottom lip.

She was in complete control, just like she liked it.

She could feel him surrender to her.

She grabbed his hands and made him squeeze her breast, guiding his touch. His mouth found her nipples quickly. His eyes looked up at her, looking for reassurance, he was pleasing her correctly. She moved his hands to wrapped around her waist, his fingers grabbing handfuls of her ass. She was so wet and turned on by his submissive demeanor. She knew, at that moment, she could make him do anything she wanted.

However, at this very moment, all she wanted was for him to be still.

She grabbed his face, a firm grip on his cheeks and told him to stop.

"Don't move." she ordered him, Jacques still hard inside her.

"Do not move again!" She commanded, her tone firm and fiery.

Jacques did as he was told.

Now that he was perfectly still, she moved her hips in small circles, moving to the motion her body needed at that very moment, making her body tingle with bliss over and over again. As she did this, she never let go of his face, never breaking eye contact.

Her words started to mumble.

*"There. No, there."*
*Passion you will never flee."*
*"My lover. Mine. You will always be mine."*
*"Even when you are inside her, Mine; you will always be."*

She could feel him pulsating inside of her, and they both released together, feeling each other cum at the same time; both bodies shivering into one another. A sensual moment, they both needed greatly.

For a few moments they held each other close, exhausted from their adrenaline rising so highly.

Between hard breaths, the first thing Jacques said was, "My wife never makes love to me like that." Colette then giggled slightly under her breath and said,

"I could have told you that."

After they both gathered themselves, they began walking towards the sounds of life and music. Jacques started to make conversation about the wind picking up, and began to ask,

"When will I see you again?"

Colette pressed her finger to his lips, bringing any questions and sounds out of his mouth to a halt.

"Soon."

"You will see me very soon." she whispered to him with her bewitching grin, he knew all too well. He returned to the tavern, and she returned home feeling satisfied and amused by her evening endeavors.

From that night on, every time Jacques entered his wife, he thought of Colette. At first, he preferred it, but after time he realized he had no control over his mind. He would close his eyes, and he was back in that forest, inside her, enthralled by her. When he made love to his wife, the heat of Colette's sexual touch flowed through him. He realized it made him a better lover, more attentive to wife's needs and pleasures. Every time they laid together as husband & wife, Colette's energy surrounded them both, as if she were right there with them. Jacques and Bernice never had sex again without both reaching their max bliss together at the same time.

Every time.

"You're welcome, plain wife."

"You're welcome."

Colette mumbled to herself often thereafter.

Chapter 8: Echoes of Intention


Janell couldn't shake the riddle from her mind:

*Take three lives and replace them with three…*
*But know this,*
*in which lifetime could it be?*
*Grow three, but not from your family tree,*
*When this happens, you will clearly see…*


See what?

Her dreams lately had been dominated by this cryptic puzzle as well as the familiar, vivid visions of her college waitressing days. Oh my, waitressing dreams. In these dreams, she was back at the Mexican restaurant—the hostess podium, the tortilla lady shaping dough off to the side, the piñatas swaying in the lobby. Every detail was exact. And every time she got *"in the weeds,"* she woke up. Too many tables, drinks for one, orders for another, a third table waiting for a chips-and-salsa refill, all while another silently judged her. It was chaotic and exhausting.

Now, the phrase "*In the weeds*" followed her to work. Her job as a social worker at the nursing home was a whirlwind of needs, emotions, and crises. Residents depended on her daily, and families leaned on her to navigate the emotional and practical challenges of aging, memory loss, and medical crises. Dementia, Alzheimer's Disease, severe memory decline—these weren't just diagnoses; they reshaped lives and strained relationships.

Some days, she felt like she was deciphering a hidden language in the way residents moved, spoke, or even avoided eye contact. A tremor in a hand, a fleeting glance, a subtle change in tone—all of it told a story. Occasionally, she caught herself wondering if her skill at reading these cues wasn't so different from something older, something almost mystical. There was a rhythm to human behavior, a pattern she could sense, if only she paid attention.

Families were a mix of devotion, guilt, and blame. Some visited rarely, criticizing small details while ignoring the care being provided. Others went above and beyond, bringing home-cooked meals and staying at mealtimes to coax their loved ones to eat. Residents remembered, judged, and responded, each interaction a new puzzle. Janell had learned to navigate them all with empathy, patience, and a quiet sense of knowing.

Even amid the chaos, she thrived. Social workers who excelled in this environment shared certain traits: charisma, subtle influence, and a knack for anticipating needs before anyone spoke to them aloud.

And there was that "social worker voice"—a tone that could calm, guide, and assert authority simultaneously.

The riddle lingered, tugging at her awareness throughout her day; Take *three lives and replace them with three... When this happens, you will clearly see...*

Clearly see what?

She would often juggle her workload and have random thoughts of her cryptic dream here and there between interactions with people.

Sometimes Janell felt that her work, so rooted in the modern, practical world, carried echoes of something older.

Patience. Observation. The ability to sense what wasn't said.

She often wondered why it came so naturally to her; the quiet knowing, the way she could feel what another person needed before they spoke.

It wasn't training. It wasn't luck. It was something deeper, as if she were remembering a language she had once known by heart.

These instincts had always come naturally, yet in recent months they felt sharper, almost charged. She wondered if it had started around the same time as the dream. The riddle whispered in the dark, strange and half-remembered, lingering each morning like salt on her tongue.

She couldn't explain why it felt connected, only that both the dream and her waking hours seemed to hum with the same invisible thread—something guiding her, though she didn't yet know toward what. But lately it had begun to feel like something awakening.

# Chapter 9: The Final Journey

Janell found herself lost in thought, as she often did these days, pondering the strange intersections of time and human understanding. If someone traveled back in time and tried to explain surrogacy; how would it go? she wondered. Imagine trying to describe a woman carrying a child for another, a child not her own, a life growing within her that shares no blood with her body. How could anyone centuries ago comprehend it? Surely, they would whisper sorcery, perhaps in awe, perhaps in fear. And maybe, in a way, there was a bit of magic in it.

Her mind wandered to her own third surrogacy journey, the final one she had committed to. For this endeavor, she returned to the very first agency she had worked with, appreciating the seamless professionalism and warmth they offered. Getting matched with intended parents was a ritual of anticipation she relished. It gave her a sense of purpose and significance. To these people, she was essential. Her womb was needed, yes—but she herself, with her strength, resilience, and presence, was equally vital.

Janell often reflected on the love languages she had explored over the years, and she recognized herself in "words of affirmation." Perhaps that explained part of her deep attachment to surrogacy; the joy she derived from knowing how deeply her actions mattered. She reveled in hearing, repeatedly, how extraordinary it was to carry a child for another. In those moments, she was more than a woman—she was a miracle worker, a creator of life in the truest sense.

Being a surrogate meant completing a family. No matter what one's past mistakes, in the eyes of the intended parents, she became an angel, an embodiment of hope and possibility. And Janell loved that role.

During her first two journeys, she had learned much from other women. Surrogacy was a sisterhood, a community of extraordinary women connected by intention. Some sought to help friends or family. Others found meaning and confidence in the process. And some, like Janell, simply adored pregnancy. Of course, the financial aspect was a practical bonus, but the emotional and spiritual resonance of the experience always outweighed it.

Janell knew, too, that surrogacy carried out controversy. Ethical, legal, and social questions surrounded the practice, particularly commercial surrogacy. Different countries and states had widely varying rules, and opinions often ran hot and extreme.

Yet she did not dwell on politics; she focused on her experience, on her life, and on the families, she would help bring into being.

Sometimes, when she sat quietly, Janell considered the subtle similarities between her work as a surrogate and her natural intuitive awareness—the kind of perception women had centuries ago. Those old seers, the palm readers, the women gifted with "sight," were in many ways early observers of human behavior, reading intentions in posture, gestures, and expression. And Janell, with her work in social services, had become a modern incarnation of that intuition. She read families, she observed unspoken cues, she understood fears and desires that were never fully voiced. In some strange, invisible way, carrying life for someone else required the same perceptive attention as divining it from subtle gestures, or foreseeing potential through observation.

Her mind returned to the essence of her role: the praise, the affirmation, the profound joy of giving life. She loved it. She thrived on it. She loved the way her body could be the vessel for hope, and the way the process required a careful, almost sacred attentiveness to detail—emotional, physical, and intuitiveness.

As she prepared to embark on this final journey, Janell felt the steady pull, a deep certainty that she was exactly where she needed to be. This was her purpose. Her calling. Her gift. Like those women of old, whose powers were whispered about and feared in equal measure, she understood that some things were greater than themselves.

She would nurture a new life, but she would also honor the invisible currents guiding her, the lessons learned from observing humanity, and the intimate dance of desire, hope, and trust that connected her to the intended parents. Every movement, every choice, every heartbeat mattered.

The final journey had begun.

## Chapter 10: A Body's Betrayal

The morning after, her cottage smelled of salt and sweat, the remnants of a night that should have left her feeling whole.

The man was gone—one of the many who found her irresistible after dark but forgettable by dawn. She heard the soft thud of the door closing, the shuffle of his boots fading into the distance.

Colette lay there for a while, skin still warm from the traveler's touch, but her heart already cold. The sheets tangled around her legs like seaweed, damp from the night's indulgence. She stared at the low beams above her bed, their edges softened by the pale gray light seeping in from the shore.

For a moment, she tried to savor the comfort of stillness. Then a sharp ache twisted in her belly. A familiar, hollow kind of pain.

She rose slowly, wrapping a thin cloth around her hips. The floor was cool beneath her bare feet as she crossed to the basin. When she lifted her linen, she saw it—deep crimson, streaking her thighs.

"No," she whispered, staring down as if the sight itself betrayed her.

"No, not again…"

The first drop of blood hit the water, blooming like ink in clear glass. The color spread, swirling, blooming outward in delicate red tendrils that reminded her of coral. The image mocked her with its beauty.

Her hands gripped the edge of the table until her knuckles went white.

"Why!" she screamed, the word tearing through the stillness of the room.

"Every month my body mocks me!"

"Man after man, and still nothing—nothing!"

She slammed her hand into the table. The basin rattled violently, sloshing water across the floor. The drops hit the boards like rain.

"Do they not leave their seed inside me like a promise? And yet…"—she looked down at herself, trembling—"…nothing grows. Nothing ever grows."

Tears burned at the corners of her eyes. She dragged her palm down the length of her stomach, smearing the blood as if marking herself with it.

"Why do you bleed for nothing?" she hissed at her own body. "Why do you ache for life that never comes?"

The cottage seemed to tighten around her, the air thick with her fury. The single candle on the table flickered, its flame stretching toward her voice as if drawn by it.

Her breath came ragged now, trembling between sobs and laughter.

She grabbed her shawl, not caring that she was still half-naked, and stormed out into the morning wind. The sea waited below, gray and endless, its waves restless against the rocks.

She stood at the cliff's edge, hair whipping across her face, and screamed into the roar of the tide.

"Why will you not give me a child?" she cried.

"I've given myself to every man who would have me—yet I am still empty! Is this my fate? To feel every desire, every flame, and bear nothing from it?"

The sea answered in waves, crashing hard against the stone. The spray stung her face, cold and sharp, but she didn't flinch.

Her blood still marked her legs, dripping into the sand as she staggered down toward the water.

"If I am not fit to create," she spat, "then I will destroy!"

She threw her bloodied cloth into the waves. The sea swallowed it whole.

Colette fell to her knees, hands sinking into wet sand, her body shaking from rage and exhaustion. The tide crept closer, licking her fingers as though tasting her despair.

A low rumble sounded from far beyond the horizon.

Thunder—or something older.

She lifted her head slowly; hair plastered to her cheeks.

The sea had gone still again, but its surface shimmered faintly, as though watching her.

"Mock me, then," she whispered hoarsely. "If I am unworthy to give life, then let my blood be the thing that wakes you."

The wind carried her words away. And somewhere beyond the breaking waves, something seemed to stir.

She stayed at the water's edge until her voice broke, until her throat was raw and the sea had taken every scream she had left to give.

The waves had gentled, their fury spent, but her own still raged within. The tide crept forward as if to soothe her cold fingers lapping at her knees. When she looked down, she saw the faint red swirl still drifting in the foam, her blood dissolving into salt.

The sight hollowed her.

When she finally stood, her legs were weak, trembling from the weight of her sorrow. She turned back toward her cottage, the wind pushing at her like a scolding hand. The shawl clung to her shoulders, heavy and damp.

Inside, the air was still cold. The man's scent still lingered with musk and sweat, fading fast. His empty cup sat on the table beside the guttered candle; wax pooled like dried tears.

She sank onto the bed, her body aching in every place that had known pleasure the night before. The linen beneath her was stained now, crimson blooming through white like a cruel reminder.

Her hands moved instinctively to her belly, pressing against the quiet there.

"There should be life," she murmured. "There should have been life."

The words broke something in her. She curled onto her side, pulling the blanket close as if she could hide from her own body.

The bleeding came steady now, rhythmic, relentless — her body releasing what it refused to hold.

She wept in silence, the sound small and desperate, swallowed by the storm still rolling far out at sea.

Hours passed. The cottage darkened.

Days followed, heavy and unmoving. Colette stayed inside, sealed away like a cocooned creature, hidden from faces, from voices, from the world that dared to continue without her.

Curtains sagged against the damp air, and a single candle guttered beside her bed, its wax bleeding down like the slow, inevitable passage of time.

She had not eaten. She had not spoken. Her body, once flushed with desire, now pulsed with the ache of betrayal. Each cramp was a cruel reminder that she was unchosen, that her womb, sacred yet silent, had become barren ground.

Her trembling hands drifted to her belly.

"Why?" she whispered.

Her voice cracked —part fury, part grief—

echoing through the dim cottage. She pressed her palms harder, as if by touch alone she could demand an answer from the body that had turned against her.

The first night passed in tears.

The next in silence.

By the third, the quiet began to change.

It wasn't comfort that came, but a strange steadiness, a voice within her, faint at first, like a hum beneath the ribs. It spoke without words, reminding her that she had survived worse storms. That her body's betrayal was not her ending, only another transformation.

She rose before dawn, opening the shutters for the first time in days. The sea glimmered gray in the distance, restless and endless, but beautiful still.

The morning breeze slipped inside, brushing her face as though to wake her.

She washed, dressed, and lit a new fire. The flame caught easily this time, as if it too had been waiting for her return.

Her reflection in the small glass above the basin startled her; pale, yes, but something fiercer in her eyes. A woman not broken but tempered.

Colette breathed deeply.

Her sorrow had not vanished, but it no longer owned her. She would step back into the world, not to seek worth in men or their promises, but to reclaim her place among the living.

The body may betray, she thought, but the spirit endures.

And when she stepped outside, the light felt warmer — the sea's call softer, almost approving.

## Chapter 11: Wings at Dawn

The morning found Colette wandering, barefoot and half-asleep, her body moving as though guided by some hidden pull. By the time she blinked herself awake, the first light of the sun was spilling across the sea, and she was standing at the edge of the Cliff of Rovona.

She lifted her arms slowly, feeling the wind sweep beneath them, imagining herself as a stork gliding over the waves. Her shoulders tilted, her chest opened to the morning air, and for a moment she could almost sense the world from above—sharp, serene, untethered.

She let herself sway with the currents, her body moving with a grace that was not entirely her own. The cliffs, the waves, the rising sun; everything sharpened and stretched in her perception, as if she were no longer standing but soaring. Her chest rose and fell with the rhythm of invisible wings, her long orange curls trailing like liquid fire in the wind behind her.

The salt spray on her face tasted like freedom; the ocean's roar filled her ears like a pulse. Steady, alive, reminding her she was still here. She could feel the tug of the tides beneath her feet, the rise and fall of the water matching the rhythm of her breath. For a moment, it was as if the sea was breathing with her.

She opened her hands to the wind, her heart lifting and dipping with the waves. In that quiet space between sky and shore, Colette felt whole again—just a woman, standing at the edge of the world, finally unafraid to feel it all.

She closed her eyes, letting the horizon blur, letting the wind move through her hair.

For one long, honest breath, she felt infinite.

# Chapter 12: Embers Awakened

Supporting emotional family members during a loved one's end-of-life care was one of the most challenging parts of Janell's job as a facility social worker. When families didn't agree with the care plan or were struggling to accept the natural process of dying, tension, confusion, and distress often followed. Today, Janell felt caught in the middle, supporting residents, the medical team, and the grieving family members, especially those who lived outside of town and were not ready to let go.

She had spent the morning essentially acting as a referee between siblings with complicated histories. When one woman started yelling at another down the hallway,

"It was your drug addictions that made mama stressed out all the time!"

Janell knew it was time to intervene.

Focusing on common ground was always her best strategy. Even when family members disagreed and repeatedly brought up negative conversations, there was usually one deep truth they shared; they loved the person who was dying. Redirecting the conversation to that shared love usually worked. As a social worker, Janell's role was to advocate for the residents, keeping the focus on their needs above all else.

Later that afternoon, Michael arrived—the devoted spouse of a resident. His wife had moved into the nursing home three months prior with advanced dementia. Every day, Michael spent hours with her before returning home, ensuring she was clean, dressed, and had enough to eat, particularly at lunch, the one meal she consistently enjoyed. Sometimes they worked on puzzles in the activity room, sometimes they sat silently in the courtyard watching birds and people go by, other times they simply sat together in her room, reliving the familiarity of their life at home.

Today, however, she was not herself. She yelled at him as if he were a stranger, telling staff to leave her alone. Michael, experienced in this pattern, gave her space. After some calming medicine and a brief nap, she finally called out for him: "Michael!! Where are you going? Don't leave me here! You always leave me!"

Tears ran down Michael's face as he tried to comfort her, reminding her he was there every day. Yet her accusations persisted.

"You do leave... I haven't seen you in so long! You're a liar, Michael! How could you leave me here? You promised you'd always love me!"

Janell watched, knowing he could no longer care for her at home physically. Once strong enough to lift lumber over his head, he now had to find strength in presence and devotion. Janell reminded him, quietly and often, that this too was a form of strength.

Being a social worker in a nursing home meant being there for the devoted family members just as much as the residents themselves.

Returning to her office with little time to regroup, Janell noticed an urgent email; the administrator was resigning. Her last day would be in three weeks, and a new administrator had already been hired. Janell braced herself for the unknown—new expectations, a different leadership style, but also recognized that transitions could bring growth.

The following week, Frederic Papon arrived to get acquainted with the staff.

Direct, confident, and commanding, he made an immediate impression.

"I've heard great things," he said to Janell. "I'd like to talk about what's working well and what needs attention."

Over the next month, his presence added a new layer to the workplace dynamic. His charm walked the fine line between harmless and inappropriate, often singling out Janell. She found herself observing his behavior, noticing how his gaze lingered a little too long, how he teased her in front of others, how he seemed to challenge her with every conversation.

Surprisingly, she didn't mind.

Amid the demands of work and home life, his attention felt like a spark, a reminder of a wilder, more reckless version of herself—a version buried under perfect posture, careful notes, and polite, quiet life.

Frederic's charisma ignited something inside Janell, a subtle fire she hadn't felt in years. She found herself replaying their conversations, thinking of comebacks, observing his movements, and feeling something messier than she should. He frustrated her, infuriated her even, but also made her pulse quicken, made her stomach flutter when he praised her work.

Maybe it was his confidence.

Maybe it was her own longing for that lost spontaneity.

Or maybe, she admitted quietly to herself, she was just human.

Drawn to the very fire she knew she shouldn't touch.

# Chapter 13: Eight Arms, One Heart

Janell had exciting news; she had been matched with her intended parents. It was simple and seemly; they had approved of each other's profiles, followed by a Zoom call, a polite exchange of greetings, and then the implicit agreement. Yes, they would work together. She had already completed the medical screenings, a thorough evaluation of everything related to pregnancy, medical history, and overall health. Blood tests, drug screenings, STD checks, Pap smears, all to ensure she was physically prepared to carry a child for someone else.

Once cleared medically, the legal phase began. The agency's attorney guided her through the contract, explaining state rules, surrogate rights, compensation, and any scenario that could arise during the pregnancy. Janell knew from experience that negotiation here was key. First-time surrogates often received lower compensation, but with her second and now third journeys, she was confident advocating for herself. She knew her value, the risks, the physical and emotional labor, and the time away from her own family. The contract was long, detailed, and unchangeable once signed. Reading it carefully, asking questions, requesting adjustments, these were essential steps to protect both herself and the process ahead.

This third journey would be different.

Janell had chosen an international family, believing it would be more business-like, with fewer hands in every appointment and daily symptom discussion. She was a busy mom, juggling three children, a household, and a career. A cartoon of an octopus mother had always resonated with her, and she often joked that her spirit animal was an octopus; eight arms to manage all the tasks life demanded. Women truly were remarkable, she thought, managing schedules, meals, homework, doctor's visits, social events, and household needs; all while maintaining their own sense of self. Pregnancy added a new layer, but it was another challenge she was prepared to meet.

Her first surrogacy had been for a single man—hesitant at first, but open-hearted once trust found its way between them.

The second was for a married couple longing to give their first child a sibling, a journey marked by cultural exchange and genuine connection.

This third would cross borders and languages, more pragmatic and carefully arranged, yet no less meaningful.

Janell felt hopeful, grounded, and quietly certain she was ready—for one last pregnancy, one final gift.

Reflecting on her life, Janell acknowledged the trials her body had endured. In her younger years, she had chosen three abortions, experiences she no longer felt the need to hide. The first two had been medication-based, early in pregnancy; the third, surgical, early but requiring a clinic procedure. These choices had shaped her, but they did not define her worth. They were part of her history, yes, but they were also proof of her resilience.

In her twenties and early thirties, she had three biological children; healthy pregnancies, full-term vaginal births and she loved them fiercely. Her surrogate pregnancies had come later, in her thirties, each bringing new life into the world for families who might never have experienced it without her. This final journey held special weight: not only did she want it to succeed, but she also needed it to succeed.

Janell contemplated the balance of her life, the delicate interplay of past and present, loss and creation. Three abortions. Three children. Three surrogacies. Life had demanded much of her body, her heart, and her spirit, and still she rose, ready to give life once more. She understood the karmic symmetry of it all: endings and beginnings, sorrow and joy, past decisions and present purpose.

This final surrogacy was more than a journey; it was her affirmation of resilience, compassion, and her capacity to create life.

And with that understanding, Janell stepped forward, fully aware of the immense gift her body was about to give.

She was ready.

## Chapter 14: A Treat for a Spider

*"Rain*

*Rain*

*Raindrops, I adore.*

*Clouds. Sun, no sun, only clouds.*

*Rain harder, harder once more."*

*"Rain*

*Rain*

*Raindrops, I adore.*

*Clouds. Sun, no sun, only clouds.*

*Rain harder, harder once more."*

Colette felt a calm energy when it rained. It soothed her, steadied her mind. She loved the sound. The smell. She watched the rain pour out of the sky for hours without moving much, just whispering these words underneath her breath. She sat cross-legged on the cottage floor, as she watched the rain, her front door wide open.

She became very fixated on a spider in the corner of her kitchen, admiring the web that latched on from one wall to the other. She was impressed by this spider's gumption and overall masterpiece.

"Hello little spider, I love the web you created."

whispering to the spider as if she didn't want anyone to hear. She carried on the conversation as if talking to an old friend.

"I have watched you for the last hour working hard. I bet you knew it was going to rain today, so that's why you built it inside. Clever spider."

"This web is your entire world, isn't it? I'm sure from the time you woke up, you have worked on it, I'm sure of it. I'm sure you got tired along the way, but you kept going, didn't you?"

Colette sighed.

"I hope you catch something today; I really hope that for you; a treat for your hard work."

"Everyone deserves a treat from time to time." Collette said to her new friend with another deep sigh.

"Yes, little beautiful spider you deserve that. You deserve a treat." Her conversation with the spider, finally coming to a halt, as she stared into the web.


Truth being told; Colette was very lonely.

Sure, when she was seen in town, she was usually the center of attention, but days like this; when she was home alone; with no one to talk to other than a simple spider in the corner of her kitchen, it made her realize how lonely she truly was. She never dreamed of a husband or having a man's arms to fall into at the end of the day. She only dreamed of a child's arms reaching out to her to be picked up. Colette wanted a child more than anything. Every time she was with a man, in the back of her mind she secretly hoped it would be the time that gets her pregnant and over time she just assumed the more men she could be with, the higher her chances were of getting that child.

But every month when her blood came, so did the sorrow to beat her down. So many men, and still no baby. She often thought she was failing at being a woman, getting pregnant shouldn't be this hard.

She continued her conversation with the spider,

"I would be a wonderful mother, you know."

"I really would."

"I would protect and adore my child. I would teach, I would listen, I would help them grow into a beautiful person."

"Why can't I be a mother little spider?" Her voice started to rise.

"Why won't it just happen for me!"

Women in this town always having another baby, only laying down with their husbands and getting pregnant. I lay down with all their husbands too, why don't they give me a baby as well?

"Damn it little spider tell me!"

"You tell me, now!"

"Do you think I wouldn't be a good mother little spider?"

65

Well?!!

Starting to pace her small cottage, Colette yelled, "I will tear down your web, tear down your world if you don't answer me!!"

Colette felt the rage build up, as it often does when she thinks about her deserving a child and still not having one at her age. She began to feel lightheaded and needed some air.

The rain had stopped.

Colette walked outside, her bare feet sinking into the wet mud that circled the stone pathway from her back door to the fields behind her home.

She noticed that Theo was home. He owned the small farm next to her cottage. Her neighbor was older, a widower that took a second wife a couple years back. He often brought Colette fresh milk and stopped by from time to time to have brief conversations about life. He understood Colette was *"different"* from the other women in town. Since all three of his girls were married off, he felt he needed to keep an eye out for Colette, checking in on her from time to time. Theo was nice looking. His long black hair was mixed with grey; his hands and arms were strong from working the farm. He ate well, his new wife was a very good cook, and they often brought Colette supper over when she would make too much.

Colette was twirling with her skirt, humming to herself, spinning like a toddler does, naive to the dizziness to come. Theo noticed Colette spinning around. She was talking to herself, barefoot in the mud, the bottom part of her long skirt wet and dirty.

Theo came close enough to where his voice could reach her.

"Colette, are you okay?" He asked with genuine concern.

Colette stopped spinning.

Paused for a moment, then looked straight at Theo.

"No Theo."

"I'm not okay."

"I'm lonely."

"I've been arguing with a spider all afternoon,"

"And I'm sad the rain stopped."


Theo looked puzzled and was not sure how to respond.

"Is there anything I can do for you?" which was the only thing he could think of saying to her in that moment.

Colette's expression changed from looking glum; to looking slightly mischievous.

"Yes Theo, there is something you could do for me; you could put a baby inside me."

Theo showed an expression of being bewildered and was not sure he heard her correctly. She had been flirtatious with Theo plenty of times, but never this direct. Colette then started walking to Theo's side of the land, her feet and legs covered in mud, her hair was down and frizzy from the weather, her skin sticky from the moisture in the air. She was covered in the sorrow and loneliness of the day and needed a man's touch to make her feel better, even for just a moment.

Now Theo was a kind man,

a loyal man

but yes, Theo was a man.

Colette started walking towards him, she looked disheveled and quite mad, her hair wild and tangled; but once she lowered her top exposing her breast in the middle of the day, Theo didn't really mind all the other things in that moment. Theo started to look around the farm to see if anyone else could see her. Only donkeys in the distance, but he didn't think they would mind much, her naked body in the afternoon.

Theo appeared slightly nervous, his first impulse was to take the rag that was over his shoulder and cover her up. He was kind in that way. By the time she was right in front of him, he could feel the pressure rising in his trousers, and his body temperature starting to rise. Even in her disarranged state, she may have been the most beautiful woman he had ever laid eyes on. Colette took him by the hand, leading him to the back shed, behind the barn.

"Miss Colette, let me get something to cover you up with, and something to eat." He said unconvincingly.

"Please Theo."

"Please."

"I need this, just for a moment." She pleaded.

She looked innocent and devilish at the same time. Her gaze was seductive to say the least, as she started to bite her bottom lip.

She then lay back on a large pile of hay. She pulled her skirt up; no undergarments were put on that morning. She spread her legs wide open. Showing Theo every inch of herself.

Theo was in disbelief this was happening.

He lived next door to Colette for years. Colette was even good friends with his youngest daughter that recently moved away. Even though his head filled with a thousand reasons he should have turned around and walked inside, he found his-self on top of her, entering her wet yearning cunt. He was hesitant at first, but she wrapped her legs around his back, making it nearly impossible for him to pull away.

He moaned hard when he first entered her.

In that very moment Colette thought of the spider. She didn't know why, but she giggled to herself, slightly.

Theo thrusted hard and placed his hand on Colette's face. He looked at her as if he was trying to remember every detail, every freckle, how many times her dark eyes blinked. For a moment, Colette felt at ease resting her cheek in his strong hand until he slid his thumb in Colette's mouth. While staring in Theo's comforting eyes, her playful nibble quickly turned into a strong bite.

"Harder Theo, harder!" she ordered.

Theo may have been older, but his body was in shape. She always knew he would make a good lover. She took Theo's hand away from her face and placed it around her throat. Her breathing became faster, which only aroused Theo more.

69

"Harder Theo!"

Her legs still wrapped around him, guiding him to thrust faster and deeper with ever motion. He tried to slow down; he was not normally the type to fuck so roughly but her legs were strong and tightened around him. Theo didn't last long before he finished inside of her. She grinded her pussy hard against him, taking every bit of cum he had to offer.

To Colette, a man's cum was the magic potion she needed to get what she wanted. To have the child, she so desperately wanted.

Theo, breathless, his body weak. Hay started to intertwine with Colette's curls and even though their interaction was only mere moments, it was just what she needed.

The two of them quickly gathered themselves, and he held out his hand to help Colette raise up to a standing position.

She then placed her hand on his cheek this time and said,

"The next time the wife makes that chicken stew I like, make sure she brings me over a cup."

He nodded, said "yes." and smiled.


Colette returned to her cottage, gathered some bread and cheese to snack on and noticed there was now a fly trapped in the spider's web.

"I see you got a treat this afternoon, as well."

She started to walk away to the back part of the cottage, shouting to her dear friend in the corner,

"Don't say anything else to me spider, I'm off to take a bath" Colette smiled, when she heard the rain start again.

## Chapter 15: Mischief and Fig Pie

It was one of those mornings that felt inspiring. The market in the old stone square was just waking up, merchants arranging their stalls, bolts of fabric, jars of honey, and hand-thrown pottery carefully placed. A new spice vendor near the fountain had set out baskets overflowing with saffron, cumin, and crushed sumac, their aromas mingling with the crisp morning air. An old woman sold olive oil in glass bottles sealed with wax and twine, giving Colette a knowing smile as she passed. Further along, a young man tended a stall piled high with dates, almonds, and sun-dried apricots, laughing easily as he offered tastes to children and travelers alike. The market wrapped around her like a familiar song.

Children darted past her, barefoot and laughing, their joy echoing between the clay-walled houses. Colette marveled at their effortless play, their exuberance spilling from them like spring water. A boy tossed pebbles behind his back and caught them, while another balanced on a broken amphora, arms stretched like sails, daring the sea breeze to lift him.

About to head back toward the fountain, something bright caught her eye: a small sunflower, its petals slightly crumpled, lay forgotten near the children's path. Colette looked up and spotted the girl who had been carrying it, skipping ahead, unaware her treasure had slipped from her fingers.

"Wait!" Colette called, hurrying over.

The girl, probably six or seven, froze as Colette handed her the sunflower. "Hey, that matches mine," she said, pointing to a sunflower wrapped around the chain at her hip. Colette shimmed her hips slightly, making the coins and metals chime together. The girl's smile bloomed wide, missing teeth and all, radiant and contagious.

Yet Colette noticed bruises; dark, fading ones and some fresh, shadowing the girl's delicate arms. The cheerful noise of the market dimmed, distant, as if echoes in a dream.

Who could hurt such a small child?

A tall, lean woman suddenly snatched the girl's wrist. Hard. So hard the girl winced.

Agnes Laflure. A gossipy middle-aged woman with a face like a frowning crow, dark hair pinned tightly, dress impeccably neat. "Stay away from her," she snapped, her voice low and cutting, glaring at Colette. "Stay away from that woman," she barked at the child, dragging her like luggage.

Anger flowed through Colette, a storm building inside her. She kept her composure, not wanting to alarm the nearby children. She looked down at the sunflower, now at her feet, bruised petals, stem broken.

A mischievous smile appeared on Colette's face. She quickly found Margot at the market. "Who is Agnes Laflure's husband?" she asked urgently.

Margot hesitated. "Henri Laflure. Overweight, gambler, often at the tavern drowning his bad luck in ale."

Colette's eyes sparkled. "I'll see you another time, Margot," she said, skipping away. Margot's question lingered in the air, unanswered; "What are you going to do?"

That evening, the sun had melted into the sea, streaking the sky with violet and gold like fading bruises. The tavern at the village edge hummed with low conversations, the clink of clay cups, and the smell of roasting lamb and old smoke. Fishermen, farmers, and merchants clustered in tired groups.

Colette entered and spotted Henri, alone at a back table, sweaty and unkempt, devouring what looked like his second or third plate of meat pies.

"Hello, Henri," she greeted.

"Hello," he muttered, wiping his mouth, unsure why she approached. He often watched Colette dancing at the tavern, observing her with more desirable men.

Colette wasted no time. "I ran into your wife today at the market. She asked me to read your fortune the next time I saw you."

"That doesn't sound like something my wife would say," Henri said, baffled.

"But she did," Colette replied, sliding onto the bench beside him, shoulder nudging his. "May I see your hand?"

Still surprised she was speaking to him, he extended it. Her fingers traced lightly over his palm, her breath soft and soothing.

"Do you like to eat, Henri?" she asked.

"I guess you can tell I do," he said, patting his stomach.

Not breaking eye contact, Colette pressed on. "What's your favorite dish your wife makes? What do you really enjoy?"

"Fig pie, I suppose," he replied.

Henri's attention shifted from pie to Colette's touch.

"You know, Henri," she whispered, "I know of something sweeter than fig pie."

With a glance around, she guided his hand between her thighs, pressing his fingers inside her. Then they moved to the back of the tavern, hidden from view by a corner and the rowdy arm-wrestling match of drunken men.

Henri's fingers slid in and out of her as she leaned back, pressing her hips forward, deepening his reach. Colette pulled his hand to her mouth, sucking his fingers while staring into his eyes.

"I taste sweet, Henri, like ripe red plums," she whispered, breathy and tempting. "Do you want to taste me?"

Henri, in trance, was captivated. He had never imagined such attention, yet he followed her every lead without question. Colette led him to a back room where chairs and candles were stored.

"Get on your knees," she commanded softly.

Henri obeyed, kissing her breast along the way.

"You're going to taste me, Henri, and not stop until I say so."

Excited and obedient, he pressed into her, tasting, exploring.

At first, he was sloppy, without much technique but she quickly grabbed a fist full of his hair and guided his mouth and tongue to the exact spot it needed to be. With his tongue pressing hard onto her clit, she slightly bounced against his face.

Pleasantly surprised, she moaned in pleasure.

*"Berries and figs go into a pie"*

*"Berries and figs go into a pie"*

Henri heard the words she begun saying but when he tried to say, "what?"

Colette jerked his face back to where it needed to be. She continued bouncing, and pressing, bouncing and pressing, her cum started dripping down his chin, but she wanted more. She wasn't going to allow him to stop until she was finished.

Colette noticed Henri started touching himself.

He pulled his dick out his of pants and started stroking it up and down. Henri was rock hard, knowing he was pleasing her and hearing her moan was the most erotic encounter of his entire life. He heard the words she started saying but could care less how insane they sounded; he was enjoying every minute and was not going to ask about the nonsense she started mumbling.

In between her moans, Colette mumbled.

*"Berries and figs go into a pie*

*Berries and figs go into a pie...*

*Be nice to others, this, a mother should know,*

*Be nice to others, you dirty old crow"*


Colette had one more climax riding Henri's tongue and Henri finished in his hand in complete exhaustion and delight.

Henri sat all the way down on the floor, while Colette leaned down beside him.

"Henri, I need you to do one thing for me."

In a blissful haze, "anything," he quickly said, trying to catch his breath.

"Soon as you get home, I want you to give Agnes a big passionate kiss. If she is asleep, you wake her up. Promise me Henri, you will do this as soon as you get home."

Henri in complete puzzlement, agreed and said, "anything you want."

Colette walked off and left Henri on the floor next to some broken beeswax candles.

Henri did as he was told that night, he woke his wife up from her sleep and without any hesitation kissed her right away. Agnes was startled at first, this was not something he normally did. She started to pull away but noticed that his kiss tasted sweet. Agnes assumed he drank too much red wine, instead of his usual ale, and figured the wine was the reason for this abnormal behavior. His kiss was passionate, using the same skillful tongue he used just hours before.

They both went to sleep that night and rested well.

The next morning and every day after, Agnes woke up with the most horrendous taste in her mouth. It became a daily torment she would learn to endure. She would spend hours drinking whatever she could take down in attempts to rid the spoiled taste. Every morning, she woke nauseous; a taste that she could only describe as spoiled crow.

Spoiled crow and fig pie.

# Chapter 16: Checkmate

"H"

Janell knew exactly what she was doing when she sent him this text.

Just the letter "H."

She sent it to get his mind wandering, *did she mean to text me? Was she really thinking of me this late? Or was it an accident?*

She was in a local lounge with her husband, a rare attempt to break their usual night routine of going to bed at 9:30 p.m. and watching TV until they passed out. It was around 11:00 p.m. on Friday, and she was on her second overpriced drink, regretting they'd gone out at all. Faking enjoyment, she secretly wished she were home in sweatpants. The music was dull, and the crowd wasn't much better. Socializing was exhausting; she had already talked to people all day at work.

She perched at the bar while her husband took another bathroom break. Scrolling through her phone, she landed on his name.

Frederic Papon—her boss.

They'd been texting earlier about a difficult family member, and she found herself rereading their conversation.

When he first started at the building, Frederic had been flirty, but their interactions had mostly become short and professional. Over the last few weeks, however, something shifted.

It began with a game of chess.

Residents started playing with the activity director, sparking conversations about who knew the game. Janell's competitive streak flared, matching her administrator's own skill and confidence. He had tricks up his sleeve, checkmating faster than she expected. Obsessed with winning, she refused to concede, and their playful rivalry grew into flirtation.

Questions about marriage and home life slowly crept into their conversations. She enjoyed getting to know him. He was newly married, seemingly in a happy relationship, but she couldn't shake the growing tension between them. She wondered if she was imagining things or enjoying the attention a little too much.

That Friday night, she sent him the "H" text. He didn't respond that night. She worried she'd made a mistake—until Saturday afternoon, when his reply finally arrived:

*"Did you mean to text me last night?"*

She responded casually, *"Nope, too many glasses of wine I guess lol."*

He replied almost immediately: *"Was just making sure the 'H' wasn't for the word Help."*

Her fingers hovered over the keys. *"Why? Would you have come to my rescue?"*

81

*"Of course,"* he answered.

*"I think I might have been a little tipsy and started to say 'Hey.'"*

*"So you were tipsy and thinking about me, huh?"*

*"Apparently,"* she texted back, cheeks flushing.

She ended the conversation, mentioning she was busy with her kids and would see him Monday. But her pulse still raced.

Why did these simple texts make her feel so flustered? She analyzed herself like any good social worker, knowing Monday at work would be… interesting.

Monday was slow, and by late afternoon, Frederic brought the chessboard to her office for another game. Their games usually took place in the living area surrounded by residents, but today the office door was open, and no one paid attention. Frederic came dressed casually in gym pants and a fitted t-shirt, his muscular upper body evident. He was more playful than usual, teasing her with a cocky grin.

"So, tell me why I was on your mind the other night?" he asked.

She kept it vague: *"I'm not sure, you were just on my mind, I guess."*

He wanted more, craving attention, while she relished keeping him on edge.

"You're not going to beat me, you know that, right?" He moved his piece slowly; his eyes locked on hers.

"I'm too good. I'm good at everything I do," he said, a faint grin tugging at his lips.

It was clear; his flirting wasn't accidental. He was teasing her, and she returned the favor by maintaining composure, letting him squirm.

"Checkmate," he announced, standing like a proud peacock.

A knock at the door saved her. He had to leave the office. She needed to regroup.

Sexual tension had been building, and it was almost unbearable.

Later that evening, at home, her phone buzzed.

One letter.

*H.*

She smiled.

So it begins.


Over the next two weeks, their flirtation escalated. Daily compliments, lingering glances, and playful texts filled her days. Walking through the nursing home felt electric, every glance and touch carrying unspoken promises.

Flirting wasn't cheating, right?

She justified it easily.

At home, her marriage lacked fire. She was often met with cold sheets and colder behavior. She needed to feel wanted, desired, and alive again.


One afternoon, at the nurse's station, she wore a tea-length skirt with flats. He approached from behind.

"Damn, you look nice today," he said, pressing close. She felt his body against hers and smelled his cologne.

She protested quietly: "Someone's going to hear you."

"So?" he shrugged. "No one heard me."

Later that day, a text arrived, *"Don't wear a skirt anymore."*

*"Why?"* she asked.

*"Because I can't focus. The only thing I can think about is running my hand up your skirt and feeling how wet you are."*

She grinned, knowing she was wearing a maxi dress the next day—appropriate, yet teasing. She loved the attention, her dormant wild side awakening.

The next day at exactly 4:30 p.m., he texted: *"I want you so bad."*

*"Prove it,"* she replied.

Seconds later, he appeared in her office, locking the door behind him.

"Stand up," he demanded.

Without a second thought, Janell stood.

She had expected him to come toward her for a kiss, but she was wrong.

He moved behind her desk, reaching past her to lift her dress to her waist. His hand slid into her panties from behind, pressing two of his large fingers inside her. She gripped the edge of the desk as he whispered into her ear.

"Damn, you're wet."

A moan escaped her lips, and she slid her hand into his pants, stroking him as he pressed against her. He carried himself like a man who was well endowed, and within seconds, his hand guided her head as he pressed her onto him. In any other situation, his forcefulness might have been alarming, but in that moment, it thrilled her. They both knew their time was limited; their adrenaline matched in intensity. Her mouth covered him briefly before they moved to the front of the desk. She pulled her panties fully down and turned, giving him a perfect view of the ass he had been watching all day.

She arched back, ready for him to enter. Her body ached for him, wanting him desperately. Pressing her hands flat on the desk, she lifted herself as tall as she could, inviting him fully.

He felt incredible—so fucking good.

She grinded back against him, both holding in moans to stay quiet. Her eyes caught the large mirror behind the desk. The man who had once infuriated her was now inside her, and for a fleeting moment, it didn't feel real.

She felt as if she were watching someone else entirely.

In the reflection, her eyes glowed a deep ember-orange—not from the overhead fluorescents, not a computer screen glitching to life behind her. It was a flare from within, a sudden ignition beneath the surface of her gaze. The light didn't shimmer; it radiated, steady and deliberate, as if some long-buried spark had finally turned its face toward daylight.

Something was watching from behind her own eyes. She could feel it, an ancient humming awareness sliding beneath her skin, threading through her nerves with a quiet, electric insistence. The sensation was sharp enough to steal her breath, potent enough to make the office around her feel too small, too quiet, as if the air itself were holding still to witness.

Was it adrenaline? Or the awakening of something she had never permitted herself to acknowledge?

Janell shut her eyes hard, as though she could lock the thing behind them—and when she opened them again, the glow had vanished. Her reflection was plain, familiar, human. But the afterburn lingered, a heat at the back of her mind that refused to settle.

He, too, was studying himself in the mirror, more intrigued by his own reflection than hers.

They shifted position. He placed his hands on her waist and lifted her onto the desk. Her ass pressed against the papers she had been working on just moments ago. Her legs curled around his strong body, and in a flash of passion, she bit his chest.

They never kissed.

She leaned back as he pounded into her. Keeping quiet was torture; she pressed her hand over her mouth. Her legs went up alongside his shoulders, and she could see from his expression that he was in complete bliss, but ravenous in his strokes. He pulled out abruptly, leaving a small mess on the office floor.

A noise at the door made them scramble. They composed themselves quickly, speaking loudly about a resident as if nothing had happened. She rubbed the evidence into the carpet with her shoe, fixed her smudged eyeliner in the mirror, and looked flushed and spent.

Her body still throbbed with desire.

When women fantasize about getting fucked on top of their work desk, it was exactly like that—every nerve on fire, every touch amplified, a delicious mix of urgency and lust, exhilarating, dangerous, and intoxicating, a forbidden escape from the monotony of routine that left her trembling and wanting more.

The following week, Janell reached out to HR and put in her two weeks' notice.

It was time to change to another building; she'd had her fun, and with a smirk, walking out felt like,

*"Checkmate."*

## Chapter 17: Inject. Rest. Repeat

The IVF medications leading up to embryo transfer are the worst part of the whole surrogacy process. No, really—the medications fucking sucks after a while.

It starts with Lupron shots in the belly. The needle is small and seems harmless at first; it doesn't necessarily hurt, but it makes Janell's moods swing like a wrecking ball. While her body adjusted, waves of heat and sweat rolled over her. For the first two weeks, she was extremely irritable. "*Moody*" didn't even come close. It was more like a pit of anger building inside her—like a tea kettle about to blow on the stove.

That was the feeling she carried all day.

Trying to stay decent in her interactions, she often apologized for snarky responses and erratic behavior. Symptoms varied, but she regularly caught herself in the bathroom mirror, taking slow breaths and reminding herself: I chose this. I chose to be a surrogate. Being this cross with the people I love isn't fair. It's not their fault I feel this way. Small pep talks became her lifeline.

During the medication phase, she became her own personal therapist, talking herself down from the ledge.

By week three, the irritability began to ease.

Then came the big-boy shots—the ones in the hip. Those hurt. After a few tries, her body got used to the sting, but her hips and upper buttocks bruised, reddened, and sometimes inflamed. Some days there was no immediate pain, but an hour later a sharp jolt shot through her hip, like a lightning bolt of medication spreading through her body.

Whatever drove her to become a surrogate, she had to keep reminding herself of it, so she didn't veer off her routine. Communicating with the fertility clinic was vital, updating them with her symptoms at every check-in. These weeks felt endless, waiting for her uterine lining to reach the perfect thickness for transfer. Sometimes the clinic adjusted meds depending on how her body responded. Her last appointment, no changes.

Things were moving along as planned.

Her phone alarm buzzed. Low. Familiar.

7:00 a.m.

Again.

Another shot.

She sat on the edge of the bed, legs dangling, body stiff. Her left hip throbbed where yesterday's injection had left a hot, red welt. Her fingers trembled as she reached for the vial. Her thoughts were louder than her movements:

This is too much.
My body isn't mine anymore.
This fucking hurts.

She took a deep breath, hand resting on the syringe. She felt like a mess of bruises, hormones, and pain. Bloated. Swollen.

Can I skip today? She wondered.
She knew she shouldn't. She was just procrastinating.
Another breath—the kind that steadied everything inside her. She prepared the shot, like she had countless times before.
She whispered: *One day closer.*

The sting made her wince. She let the pain sit inside her. Even in the ache, even when giving up sounded easier, she knew what was coming was bigger than her discomfort. Some days the needle went in slower, not because she hesitated, but because her skin had grown thick and sore, like leather.
Red. Angry. Swollen.

She had tried icing before and after, rotating sides like they said. The oil-based medication sat heavy under her skin; she could feel it spread. An hour or two later, nausea crept in. By noon, her head pulsed with pain, her breasts tender and heavy, and her thoughts moved sluggishly, lost somewhere in the blur of hormones.

Mood swings came out of nowhere. A commercial made her cry. An email made her snap. Every sound felt like a personal attack. She caught herself squeezing her fists, not because it helped the pain, but because she was pissed off.

Her body hurt.

Really hurt.

No one got it.

She was tired of pretending it was fine. Her skin was on fire, her stomach bloated like a drum, her moods flipping from sadness to rage without warning.

Just breathe.

You can get through these next couple weeks.

This third time—why did it feel longer? Harder?

Then the intended parents' translator texted her:

*"You're amazing for doing this! Keep it up—almost to embryo transfer day ❤☐"*

She wanted to throw her phone. She almost did.

They didn't see this part. The nausea at 10 a.m., sobbing at 2 p.m., snapping at someone chewing too loud at 4:30pm, lying in bed with a heat pack and guilt at 8pm. They saw a "selfless surrogate"—not a woman hijacked by hormones.

Pain played tricks on her mind. In that moment, she felt angry at the intended parents. They didn't feel the oil burning under her skin, the soreness that lingered no matter how many times she switched hips or iced. They didn't know how exhausting it was to live in a body that didn't feel like hers anymore.

So, she squeezed her fist. Hard.
It was the one part of her not swollen, not aching, not drugged.
And yes, she was irritable, angry, tired of being polite.
But still, she did it.

She sent back a text: smiley face emoji. *Almost to the big day!* Heart. Heart. Another fucking heart.
Inject. Rest. Repeat.
For weeks, this was her life. She carried someone else's dream while carrying her own exhaustion.

This is strength.

Not glowing and grace, but clenched fists, swollen hips, and showing up anyway.

This is being a surrogate.

## Chapter 18: A Pirate's Allure

Colette was enjoying a productive morning cleaning her small cottage, she had all her shutters open and felt herself part of the birds' conversations outside her windows. On the outside, her cottage was covered in moss, with ivy creeping up the weathered stone walls. Inside, low beams crossed the ceiling, and herbs hung in neat bundles.

Sage, rosemary, and thyme.

Filling the space with a soothing, earthy scent.

Colette sat at her spinning wheel, working on a large basket of wool, humming to herself. She now listened to the buzz of a bee that had managed to get inside. Her rhythm of humming and spinning was soon interrupted by a pounding knock at the front door, making her jump. She rose and crossed the worn floorboards to the door, unlatched it, just as Margot burst in, nearly stumbling over the threshold. Winded and wide-eyed, Margot's cheeks were flushed with urgency. Colette's face reflected frustration; her friend had interrupted a pleasantly peaceful morning in such a manner.

Margot had become the closest female friend she had in many years.

"Have you heard the news?" Margot leaned in closer. "Tall ships, black sails—they came in just past dawn; bold as anything. The buccaneers have taken shore. Have you seen them yet?" She spoke quickly, her excitement evident.

Colette raised an eyebrow, half-skeptical, half intrigued.
"Pirates, Margot? Really?"
"Apparently, they're only here for a week or so, to buy and trade. I also heard the entire crew isn't bad looking."
"Then, there is the captain. Alluring, they say."
"Apparently he's a real sight to see, a voice like honey and thunder."
Margot tugged at Colette's sleeve like a child urging her toward mischief.

Colette stared at her anxious friend for a moment, then slowly glanced at the spinning wheel, the wool, and the stillness of her cottage. Margot hoped for a much more enthusiastic response.
Colette's mood had been up and down lately, and Margot hoped the news about the men would lift her friend's spirits.

"We need some excitement tonight; there are several musicians on board, and I'm sure they'll be at the tavern later." Margot had grown up with strict parents and had never been allowed to dance or sing. Since both her parents passed last winter, she had finally started coming out of her shell. She loved the carefree spirit Colette brought out in her, but this sad, melancholy Colette was not the friend she wanted tonight.

"You're not getting ill, are you?" Margot asked with true concern.

Colette agreed to meet her later and blamed her mood on lack of sleep. "Let me nap this afternoon. Rest is essential. I don't intend to meet dashing pirates with dark circles under my eyes and a yawn on my lips."

She led her friend out the yellow cottage door and waved goodbye, returning to her humming—disappointed the buzzing bee was now gone.

The village was lively that evening with the new arrivals. Music spilled from the tavern—lively fiddle reels and the rhythmic thump of boots on wood, mingled with laughter and the clinking of mugs filled with ale. By the time Colette arrived, rested and radiant, the tavern was packed with broad-shouldered sailors with sun-darkened skin and strange accents telling stories of their journeys.

Colette spotted Margot immediately, clearly having met someone. Margot called out, "Colette, come over here!"

She was sitting at the table, a couple of drinks in, her bosoms pushed up high. Colette had never seen her friend like this and loved it.

"Colette, this is Louis," Margot introduced her new companion. Louis was very desirable, with a sultry appearance. Polite and a little shy compared to his thunderous crewmates; he seemed almost approachable.

Everyone began clapping and yelling "OPA!"

Apparently, the captain had just walked in. He stood apart from the chaos, leaning against the doorway with the casual authority of someone used to being obeyed.

Colette had been in a strange mood most of the day, but when she laid eyes on the captain, her mood quickly shifted. He might have been the most handsome man she had ever seen—tall, strong, adorned with beautiful jewelry and leather. His hair was long and braided uniquely, shells and metal rings intertwined. She observed how everyone interacted with him; he was funny, charming, mesmerizing. He noticed Colette watching and did the polite thing by introducing himself.

"I'm Captain Julien. I don't believe we have met yet."

"I'm Colette," she said, attempting eye contact, but failed.

He carried the scent of salt and something darker.

Clove, perhaps, and smoke. He smiled and continued his conversations. Colette wasn't used to being overlooked. Slightly disheartened, she continued to watch him.

Louis pulled out a worn fiddle; his fingers flew across the strings with effortless joy, summoning sound that was wild, alive, and impossible to ignore. A slightly drunk Margot grabbed Colette's hand, their coin scarves tied snug at their waists clinking in rhythm. Villagers and sailors alike gathered around them.

They danced, laughed, and drank ale.

Louis' eyes never left Margot as she winked at him, twirling. Everyone in the tavern had eyes on the two of them—everyone but the captain.

Colette tried to catch his attention but was disappointed most of the evening.

Margot asked, "What do you think of Louis?"

"Handsome, right?"

Colette agreed but was slightly distracted.

She reassured Margot that tonight was about fun—Louis was talented and yes, very handsome. Margot was pleased but then realized her friend might also like Louis. She pushed the thought aside, focusing on dancing, laughing, and feeling alive.

Louis invited them back to the ship for the evening to try some exotic wine. Colette tried to decline politely, not wanting to overshadow her friend, but Margot insisted.

Colette slipped outside, looking for fresh air.

Outside, near the fire, Colette found Pascal—a man carving a small wooden bird.

"Is that for me?" she asked flirtatiously.

"I can make one for you, but this one's a toy for the captain's boy," he replied softly.

Colette learned Captain Julien had twin sons, ten years old, clever and loud, still aboard the ship. She admired Pascal's gentleness as he carved the bird, the slow, intentional strokes, and the reverent attention he gave to his work.

"Why a stork?" she asked softly.

Pascal smiled. "It's not flashy, like a falcon or hawk.

It carries meaning. Something quiet, something sacred."

Colette enjoyed listening to him speak, a calm contrast to the tavern's chaos.

However, their conversation was interrupted by a loud, drunk Margot.

"Colette, you must come with me!" Margot ordered. Her lips were stained with red wine. "Please, come hang out with me and Louis. I'm worried I'm not experienced enough for him—what if he wants me to do something and I'm not sure what he means?"

After waving goodbye to Pascal, Colette walked back with Margot onto the ship, noticing its impressive size. Once they found Louis, Colette realized how awkward the two were alone; obviously why they wanted her around.

A shirtless Louis, his chiseled chest marked with black markings, filled the space with a magnetic presence. Colette tried hard not to show him the kind of attention she felt, fearful it would upset Margot.

"Margot tells me you're a palm reader," Louis said.
"Will you read mine?" he asked.

Colette sat beside him, and Margot immediately joined her. She reached for his hand, lightly caressing his palm, when she noticed Margot pressing kisses along the back of her neck.

"Margot, what's gotten into you tonight?" Colette murmured. Her breath was warm and sweet with wine.

"Go on, Colette. Tell him his fortune. Don't mind me," Margot said, attempting seduction, clearly putting on a show for Louis.

All night, Colette had seemed *off*; the captain showed no interest. She decided to let it go and enjoy this new, daring side of her friend. With Louis's devilish smile in front of her and Margot kissing her neck, rubbing her shoulders, Colette felt a heat stirring inside her.

"Pass me that wine, Louis," she said, comfortably directing him.

She could feel Margot's large breast pressing against her back as the kisses continued. Knowing Margot was unsure how to proceed beyond kissing, Colette guided her friend's hands down to her own breast. Louis leaned back, unraveling the leather strings on his pants. He tugged at the patterned cloth covering Colette's hair.

"What are you hiding under here?" he asked.

Margot quickly replied, "She has the most beautiful orange hair; I don't know why she always keeps it hidden." Both urged Colette to reveal it. In one seductive motion, she removed her top and headscarf, letting her long orange curls cascade over her breasts.

Louis stared, captivated by her exposed beauty.

Colette, sensing his desire, insisted Margot kiss her immediately. Clumsy and playful, Margot fell between them. Colette drank more wine to match her friend's reckless wildness.

Louis began removing Margot's top; her large, curvy breasts bounced enticingly. Their eyes locked, both realizing the electricity of the moment. Colette reveled in his dark sexual aura, enjoying his company.

Louis attended to Margot's right breast while Colette focused on the left. They kissed, sucked, and nibbled her friend's flesh— pleasure Margot had never known before. She had only been with two men in her life, and both were painfully dull. Her moans grew loud and unrestrained.

Louis stripped completely naked, hard and ready. Colette felt temptation but held back, wanting Margot to revel in him. She directed him to lie across the bed, furthest from her, and nudged Margot toward him. She watched as Margot mounted him, sliding in and out, both moaning with exhilaration.

Colette's body pulsed with arousal. One hand of Louis held Margot's waist, steadying her on top of him; the other gestured Colette forward.

"Come here. I can please you too," he urged.

He pulled her down, inviting her to ride his face. Colette removed her skirt, letting her pussy meet his lips. Facing Margot, the two girls kissed, an intoxicating combination of pleasure and desire.

Louis, experienced and attentive, simultaneously pleased them both.

He had remarkable stamina, exploring many positions with Margot—on top, standing, bent over, tasting and being tasted. Throughout, he watched Colette, noting her appreciation.

He tried multiple times to enter her, but she refused. She wanted him to focus on Margot first. Between exotic wine and mounting tension, the sexual atmosphere tormented her. Fingers and tongues weren't enough; she craved penetration.

Eventually, Margot collapsed, exhausted, leaving Colette alone with Louis.

He kissed her passionately. She resisted at first, then gave in, tasting him, pressing his fingers inside her, grinding against them.

Her body quivered; she needed him to enter her.

"Stop kissing me like that, or I'm going to fuck you," she warned.

Louis laughed, assuming she was teasing.


"Margot's exhausted. I have more to give. Let me give it to you," he said, pressing his hard cock against her thigh.

His gaze was magnetic, her pussy throbbing, wanting him, but thoughts of her friend held her back. She grabbed him by the throat, pushing him away.

Surprised, Louis laughed at her strength.

"Where is Pascal's chamber?" she asked.

Louis pounded on the ships' wall.

He hollered out, "Manny, go get Pascal."

"Who the hell is Manny? and was he listening to us the whole time?"

Colette didn't even care, her vision was starting to become blurred, her body pulsating as heat coursed through her veins. Soon as Pascal got to the room, he noticed her panting and reaching out for him. A rejected Louis, got behind Margot, mounting her like an animal.

Colette was so turned on, so intoxicated with foreplay.

Without hesitation, she pulled Pascal into the room and told him, "I need you to Fuck me."

She took off his shirt quickly, he was not as muscular as Louis, but his dick was hard and that's all she needed in that moment. She helped him untie his pants faster. She was pulsating uncontrollably now. She just needed him to enter her, or she was going to explode. She pulled him on top of her and climaxed almost immediately.

Louis observed from the corner, glass of wine in hand, admiring the scene. Margot remained unconscious. He stroked himself, with competitive desire gleaming in his eyes. Pascal was holding his own.

Colette shifted positions, riding Pascal while on his back now, massaging her breasts, while locking eyes with Louis across the room. He had seen many women, yet he was mesmerized by her sexual freedom.

Both felt the same hunger.

Even with Pascal inside her, she still wanted more.

Louis approached, fingers sliding down her back, finding the crack of her ass, and easing a finger inside.

This was new, she thought.

Glancing at Margot, she laid still, asleep, Colette then nodded to Louis.

She thrust back, riding Pascal while feeling Louis's finger deep inside her ass.

The pleasure was exquisite.

Still thrusting on top of Pascal, she pulled Louis close, kissed him, biting his bottom lip, and whispered "you know what I want, don't you?"

Then taking his cock into her mouth, making it slippery.

He replaced his finger with the tip of his dick, entering her ass gently.

Pascal, near his limit, was complemented perfectly by Louis's rhythm.

The three moved together in perfect harmony.


Pascal inside her, Louis inside her.

All three moaned.

All three felt their bodies tingling and reached climax together.

## Chapter 19: Mothers in the Balance

The new job is going great. Everyone has their specific roles, and it was organized, much more organized than the last building. Hower, Janell quickly discovered that while it might be a different building, she was consumed with the same issues. The physical layout had changed, the logo on the badge was new, but the emotional terrain was still the same. Every nursing home had its own song, same repetition, but each with its own tempo, people, small victories, and emotional exhaustion.

Overall, this new building was a positive change, for many reasons.

*Many reasons.*

Yet, no matter the building, staff were stretched thin, policies were vague and often bent. Sometimes it took something major to make one focus again, fully.

This week, a man came to visit one of the residents. Staff assumed he was a visitor or volunteer. He blended in—friendly, seemingly harmless. A resident who was often confused insisted that "*the man*" was looking for something and got angry when he couldn't find it. At first, one might assume her delusional thoughts were spilling out, but another resident reported seeing *the man* rummaging through her nightstand drawers. Janell couldn't let it go. Being new, she needed to know more. Security cameras showed this visitor interacting with several residents. Families were contacted, but no one knew him. She discovered the unknown visitor was signing under different names, and further camera footage exposed him kissing a resident on her mouth. She looked confused—not resisting but not engaging either. Janell felt a rush of adrenaline and disgust.

As she interviewed other residents, she discovered the same man had tried to kiss someone else. Anger surges strong emotion that could awaken any healthcare worker, especially a social worker. Police intervened, and appropriate actions were taken.

Abuse and neglect could also be subtle. Janell trained herself to notice patterns, residents wearing the same clothes every day, missing hygiene care, rushed or rough interactions from staff. CNA turnover was constant. Some new aides meant well, but they rushed through rounds as if racing an invisible clock. No bruises, no yelling—just coldness, impatience, a tray dropped too hard, a sigh when asked for help, muttered words like "you're fine" when someone said they were cold.

Janell documented it all, reported quietly and carefully, followed up on investigations, but wondered how many soft cries were dismissed, how many cold meals went uneaten. Abuse was often the absence of something: warmth, patience, dignity. At the end of the day, better policies, training, and systems were essential. Anger—strong, righteous—kept her awake, vigilant, and aware.

Some days, Janell went home emotionally drained.

She tried to vent to her husband, but he didn't fully understand the dynamics of her work. Physically present, she was often emotionally distant. Absorbing sorrow and managing conflicts at work left her weighed down.

One evening, standing at the sink, scrubbing a pan for dinner, the weight felt heavy in her hand. She muttered complaints about no one defrosting anything, frustrated by the small domestic tasks. Her husband entered, clearly irritated by her tired demeanor.

"I had a long day," she said quickly.

He grabbed ice and mumbled as he left the kitchen, "It's always a long day."

The words weren't cruel. That's what made them sting.

They were true.

Later, the steam from her daughter's bath began to cool. Bubbles clung to the edge of the porcelain, and the bubblegum scent of bodywash was nostalgic. Janell zoned out, staring at the wall, catching a glimpse of her tired face in the mirror.

"Mom," her daughter whined, "you didn't bring the purple towel."

Janell closed her eyes for just a second.

"You know I like the purple one, mom."

"Mom."

"Mom, I want the purple one," her daughter insisted, splashing water against the tile.

Janell's head snapped up. "It's just a towel. Just use the one I gave you."

"The purple one is softer," her daughter said, her small voice defiant yet fragile.

"Mom!"

"Jesus, just take the towel I gave you!"

The sharpness in her voice surprised even her.

She quickly apologized.

"Mommy's just tired from work. Do you want to watch Disney Plus? A movie maybe?"

Her daughter hugged her knees and looked away, shrugging. The quiet dripping from the faucet filled the bathroom with tension.

How could she feel so drained that her own child's small needs felt overwhelming? Her thoughts made her feel worse. The snappiness at home was becoming frequent. Her family didn't understand the nonstop rollercoaster she faced daily; the grief, the conflict, the responsibility, all absorbed in her role as a social worker.

Mom guilt was heavy and relentless. She gave so much at work, then felt like she had nothing left for home. She reminded herself of the small wins; hugging her kids before bed, answering a question despite her fatigue, saying "I love you," and promising to get up and do it all over again tomorrow. That had to be enough.

Tomorrow will be a better day.

As long as no one asked her, *"What's for dinner?"*
Five minutes after walking through the door, it would be a better day,

She told herself this, as she drifted off to sleep.
Her dreams soon followed with the cryptic riddle she knew all too well.

*Take three lives and replace them with three…*
*But know this,*
*in which lifetime could it be?*
*Grow three, but not from your family tree,*
*When this happens, you will clearly see…*

## Chapter 20: Conjuring My Own Magic

The embryo transfer day had arrived.

This was the big day, everything Janell had been preparing for, the shots, the pills, the bloating, the hormonal chaos, all of it. She needed everything to go perfectly.

She woke up early, not out of obligation, but because her body was already alert, buzzing with something that wasn't quite exciting and wasn't quite fear.

Just...heaviness.

Janell, in bed for a moment, hand resting on her stomach.

It didn't feel magical.

It felt tender, a little tight, as if her body already knew what was coming and was bracing for it. She wanted to feel joy, hope, something cinematic but instead, she mostly felt the pressure.

What if it didn't work?

With her first two surrogacies, the embryo transfer had succeeded on the first try, thank goodness. She needed this one to succeed on the first try as well; the thought of postponement, more months of medication, this thought made her feel as if she might give up, if it didn't take.

She drank the water the clinic instructed her to; by the time she arrived, her bladder was screaming. A full bladder helped with the transfer. The white walls, the quiet voices, the hopeful energy in the air; it all felt familiar and surreal today.

At the clinic, they gave her something to calm her nerves, a Valium, just like the other times. The procedure was much like a normal pap smear, feet in stirrups, knees falling to the sides. Under the fluorescent lights, Janell lay exposed, open, trying not to let her knees shake. Usually, she would find something in the room to focus on, but this time, she closed her eyes.

She took deep breaths. She pictured herself pregnant again. She imagined herself as a beautiful, glowing fertility goddess, like the maternity photos you can often find on Pinterest. Usually, a woman cradling a perfectly round belly, flowing fabrics rippling in the imagined wind.

Her mind wandered to the compensation. With her first journey, she had debated discussing the money, wanting to come across as a woman who simply loved being pregnant, participating in an amazing journey.

That was true—but would she be on this table, legs spread, knees trembling, if she weren't getting paid?

This third time, she thought of it as a second job. And, in her opinion, making humans wasn't the worst side job; delivering a miracle for a deserving family while supporting her own family financially.

A win-win.

Then it happened.

They brought in the embryo, a microscopic possibility, and guided it into her uterus.

A whisper of hope and science.

Janell watched the monitor, heard the soft, practiced voices of the team, felt her heart pounding. And then—it was done.

Janell stayed still for a few minutes afterward, not because the embryo could *fall out* but because the moment felt too important to rush.

It was inside her now—someone else's baby, possibly. She closed her eyes tightly and clenched her fist, not from pain but from all the unspoken emotions coursing through her.

She breathed slowly, conjuring her own internal magic to take root.

The doctor's orders were to relax with her feet up for a couple of days and wait to take a pregnancy test.

The days afterward

—the quiet space, the in-between, the waiting—these days are strange. Janell analyzed every tingle, every flutter, every mood shift. She swung between hope and detachment like a pendulum. No one warns you about how lonely this part can be, how often she held her breath from exhaustion, fear, and hope all at once.

Within a few days, she noticed subtle symptoms. Cramping, not like period cramps but a light pulling in her lower abdomen. She told herself it could be implantation, but it could also be the progesterone.

She felt more tired than normal. Bone-deep fatigue made it difficult to stay awake; even stopping at a red light could leave her eyes heavy. Her body craved naps.

The scents around her seemed stronger, more pronounced. Coffee tasted slightly off; her breasts felt tender in the mornings. She questioned whether it was real or her mind playing tricks because she wanted this so badly.

She tried to listen to her intuition, her loyal inner guide, always whispering the truth she already knew.

The longest ten days finally passed.

Janell's heart swelled with accomplishment when the second blue line appeared. The pregnancy test clearly showed a positive result. She inspected the small piece of plastic from every angle, seeking certainty. Letting the intended parents, the clinic, and the surrogacy agency know was more than exciting, it was gratifying.

Choosing Janell as their surrogate had been the right decision.

Her body was capable. The positive pregnancy test gave her the boost to endure the remaining medications and injections, despite her bruised hips. A sense of purpose radiated through her entire body.

She thought of life now growing inside her.

She felt her personal aura strengthen, her senses heightened, mother -nature's essence overflowing her being. A metamorphosis was underway, as if she were transforming into something extraordinary.

Pregnancy made her feel powerful.

And it had begun.

# Chapter 21: Sweat, Sweetness and Apricots

Colette's eyes snapped open as sunlight pierced through the shutters of her cottage. The fog of sleep clung to her, but already she was fighting it, forcing her lids to shut tight again. She wasn't ready to let go of the dream.

Her dream had been perfect that night. Magical.

Beneath her patchwork quilt, she pressed her eyes shut harder, willing herself back. She could almost hear them still—three children laughing in the tall grass behind her cottage, their voices sharp and sweet as they called out, *Mama.*

Two boys and a baby girl.

Her children.

In this dream, the children had olive-toned skin and curls in shades of chestnut and sable. Magic clung to them like a second skin, woven into their being as naturally as laughter.

The girl, wild as fire.

Her hair sprang in every direction, honey eyes that dared the world to deny her. She knelt in the garden beds, small hands buried in soil, whispering to the roots. She pressed her palm against a dying tree, and it bloomed.

The middle child, a boy, was tied to wind and sky. He ran faster than the breeze, his laughter carried by every gust, Birds followed him, feathers spiraling in his wake. He would whistle a tune that shifted the direction of the wind

The eldest, her firstborn son in this magical dream, carried the rain. He summoned mist to soothe scorched earth, and when his feet struck the ground, it was as if the rhythm of his heart called down the storm. The joy she felt in her dream was so fierce it terrified her. To feel that much happiness, to feel her soul stretch wide enough to contain it.

It left her trembling.

And then it was gone.

She woke, alone. Again.

A hollow ache clawed under her ribs. It was a strange agony, mourning children who had never been born. Missing voices never spoken. Longing for kisses that had only lived in her imagination. And yet, the love she felt for them was real. As real as the dirt beneath her fingernails, as the wood beams above her bed.

Her throat tightened. She whispered to the silence, to the gods, to no one and to everything,

"Why show them to me, if I cannot have them?"

Her voice broke, then became a scream.

"WHY WON'T YOU LET ME BE A MOTHER!?"

Her fury rattled the cottage, a clay pot toppling and shattering as her cry echoed against the stone walls.

Breath ragged, she stood in the stillness that followed. Her voice rasped when she muttered to herself,

"Not today. Not again. I need to get out."

She spoke to the madness, the silence, the unseen viewers in the corners of her small home.

And with a feral certainty, Colette made her decision.

If she couldn't have children, then she would have pleasure.

Not love. Not tenderness. She didn't want to be held or promised anything.

She wanted to burn.

She wanted sweat and heat, to feel weight pressing her into the earth until her screaming inside went quiet. She wanted lust to drown her grief at that very moment.

Pacing the cottage, muttering under her breath, words began to tumble out, harsh and raw.

*"Sweat. Smell. Sweat. Smell. Sweat. Smell."*

She repeated the words until her jaw ached, until she growled aloud, like an animal caught in its own skin.

Grabbing her cloak, she stormed out her yellow-painted door, sandals slapping the dirt, her face lit harshly by afternoon sun.

The village greeted her with noise, scents, the press of bodies. She was hungry, lust clawing at her, but her stomach, too, ached from emptiness.

The smell of cinnamon caught her first.

Bread. Warm, spiced, beckoning.

She followed it into the bakery.

The baker was there—an ordinary man with flour-dusted arms, forearms strong from kneading dough. He nodded at her, unaware of the storm that walked through his door. He was decent, pleasant, and utterly unremarkable. His smile was nice, but it was the bread that attracted her attention.

Colette sat, savoring warm bread with jam that nearly melted on her tongue. She wondered, idly, if the baker would do. If he could smother the fire.

Then—

"Alice, grab more rags!" the baker called.

A girl emerged from the back.

Colette froze.

Wispy blonde hair, apron dusted with flour, eyes sharp and dark against pale skin. Thin, almost too thin for someone surrounded by pastries, and yet the rawness of her beauty struck like a blow.

Her name was Alice.
And instantly, Colette's fire sharpened into focus.

The ache that had been wild and formless now had a face.
The girl cleaned the table beside her. Their eyes met.

"Hello," Colette said, her voice velvet.
"I'm Colette. I know almost everyone here, but not you."

"I'm not from this village," Alice snapped, scrubbing harder. Her tone was sharp, her body language clear, she owed no one explanations.

The baker sighed from behind the counter.
Alice relented, with obvious irritation. "I'm his niece. I don't like it here. Glad to be leaving soon."
Colette's lips curved. She admired the girl's rudeness. Sharp edges were more interesting than dull kindness.
"No worries. I don't always like it here either," she replied softly, watching her move.
And Alice was watching her, too.
Desire tangled in the air.

Colette's mind painted the girl already—messy hair, lips swollen, gasping under her. She bit her bottom lip, muttering again under her breath, low and rhythmic.

*"Sweat. Smell. Sweat. Smell."*

Her gaze caught Alices.
Not a command. Not a plea.
A pull.
Alice's lips quirked. "Are you still hungry?"
Colette nodded.

"Come with me," Alice ordered.
The words struck like sparks.
Colette followed her into the back without hesitation.

The air was thick with the scent of simmering soup, herbs and smoke wrapping around them. A cauldron bubbled over fire, filling the room with humid heat.

Alice scooped a spoonful, blew softly across it, and held it out. "Taste."
The command was sharp, thrilling.
Colette obeyed slowly, deliberately.

123

The soup slid warm down her throat.

Alice turned to fetch a bowl, but Colette grabbed her wrist.

The girl didn't pull away. Instead, she stepped closer.

Their gazes locked, heat pooling in the air between them. Sweat glistened across Alice's brow.

"You smell like apricots," Colette whispered, voice husky.

"I love the taste of apricots."

Alice didn't hesitate. She crashed forward, her mouth claiming Colette's with force. Her tongue pressed deep, tasting her, devouring her.

For the briefest flicker, Colette thought of Margot—the pirate ship, the one other night she had kissed a woman.

But Alice was different. Fiercer. Hungrier.

Colette moaned, her hand tangling in Alice's pale hair, pulling her closer, breasts pressed against breasts. Their linen blouses were little more than teasing barriers.

Usually, Colette needs a man inside her to make her cum, but this Alice, this passionate, assertive Alice, with her sweat that smells sweet like apricots, was making her cum in mere minutes. Alice fucked Colette with her fingers right there on the tabletop that so many delectable pastries had been made. Alice was rough and unforgiving; she charmingly had flour on her cheek. Colette giggled sightly, like she usually does after a good climax. Giggling at the sight of it all, feeling satisfied. Pulling her face away from this stranger's tasty kisses, Colette whispered "I want you to cum too." "Let me taste you."

Colette stood up away from the table, she grabbed this thin Alice and laid her back.

She pulled Alice's apron off, she wanted to feel how wet she was, what her pussy felt like. Colette's fingers entered Alice, she was tight and wet. She fucked her with her fingers and then found her tongue entering her soon after.

She knew she would taste like apricots.

Everything about this Alice was sweet, her soup, her sweat, her body.

The girls heard voices coming toward the back room they were in. They laughed, while kissing each other again, getting their clothes back on quickly. They wiped flour off their faces and each other's backs and shoulders.

Alice's uncle walked into the room to find them both dipping pieces of bread into the soup. Staring at one another, they tried not to laugh.

"Alice, I need your help up front." The baker said to his niece, oblivious to the aroma of passion in the moist air.

"Be there in one moment," she told him.

"Come back tomorrow," Alice ordered Colette as she walked her out of the shop. As she passed by Alice's uncle, she gave him a quick wink; unsure why, she never noticed him before today. Her sexual escapade in the back of his shop had her now in a very flirtatious mood. A much better mood than she was experiencing that morning.

The next day came.

Colette was in the mood for that delicious soup and Alice's sweet kisses. She soon found out that Alice had left early that morning to return to her home village. Colette, at first disappointed to hear this news then smiled at the thoughts of yesterday.

She was toying with me the whole time, she knew she was leaving today.

That cheeky Alice.

That sweet stranger Alice.

Colette fucked the baker that day instead.

On the same table, in the same hot room next to the fire with the soup boiling. Soon as the last person left the shop, she walked over to the baker, with a pouty, flirty presence and said,

"Show me the back room, let's make sure the soup taste like it did yesterday."

Colette, still a little bummed Alice wasn't there, told the baker directly to his face once they entered the back room, "I'm going to kiss you, then you're going to fuck me, when we are done, don't speak to me, okay?" Which was more of a demand instead of a question.

The kisses weren't as sweet.

The sweat was not as sweet, but the baker's dick was hard and stayed hard for an impressive amount of time. She leaned over the table and let him enter her from behind. She came as soon as she closed her eyes and thought of Alice's perfect small breast, and how wet she was when her fingertips were inside her. With Colette's ass bouncing against the baker, deep inside, a steady deep motion, he filled her with his cum.

Colette, entertaining herself, giggled at the thought of the cream filled pastries in the front window. The baker, breathing heavily, pulled out and walked back to the front of his shop.

Colette felt the need to run her finger through the flour on the table and wipe it on her cheek.

She giggled again slightly.


She then grabbed a loaf of bread and a bowl of soup and bought some apricots at the market before returning home for the day.

The fire inside her was quiet, for now.

Chapter 22: Speaking Through Touch

Janell pulled into the same parking spot she always did, the same cracked pavement greeting her tires. Another morning, the same déjà vu feeling she always got when reaching her job. She walked through the front doors, offering her automatic "hello" five times in a row, each one as practiced and predictable as the day before. It was going to be a long day, like most days. On top of a new admission with a panicked daughter, a nurse reported two falls with no injuries this morning—families quick to blame. Janell also overheard a staff dispute over a schedule change and the maintenance guy mentioning he was about to do a practice fire drill.

And of course, it was care plan day.

Oh, Wednesdays.

Wednesdays were for care plan meetings with long-term care residents and their families. Supposedly a quarterly update to discuss changes in care, new developments in the building, and resolve any issues. Most of the time, though, the fifteen-minute pow-wow turned into a complaint festival. And Janell was over it.

From today's meetings, the complaints were as follows:

*"I bought Mom six really nice matching outfits from Dillard's and now she only has two sets in her closet. And no, I didn't put her name on anything—no one told me to."*

It's common sense, Janell thought.

At home, she lost socks and shirts all the time in a household of five. This building had over a hundred residents. And she didn't even want to think about the reimbursement requests, or the missing receipts that would soon follow.

Next complaint: *"Dad says there's a night aide who's really rude. She comes in, doesn't say her name or what she's doing, and rushes him. He mentioned this about three weeks ago."*

Umm... Lady, that was three weeks ago. How was she supposed to follow up on that?

Another One: *"Mom is missing her glasses, again. Why does the staff not keep up with her things? This is ridiculous."*

Janell politely reminded her that her mother wanders the building all day, self-propelling her wheelchair up and down the halls. The last time the glasses went missing, they were found in another resident's room, but sure, blame the staff.

And her favorite complaint from the day. *"Why can't my mother sit at the popular table in the dining room?"*

The popular table?

What did these families want from her? Popular tables? Really.

By noon, care plans were usually over, and Janell's mind drifted toward lunch. Then she heard it.

"Help me!"

"Help Me!"

"Help me!"

A man yelled repeatedly in the living room area. Two nurses glanced up from the nurse station. He was fine, just hollering again; unable to explain exactly what he needed. Lately, it has been more frequent, louder.

He leaned back in his chair, staring at the ceiling.

"Help me! Help meeee!" His words cut through the calm room like a sudden winter wind. A nurse tried to ask questions; he couldn't respond too. The mind he'd lived with for over ninety years had turned against him, twisting light into danger and strangers into ghosts.

A med aide offered water, but he swatted it away. "Help me!!!!" He thrashed his head, letting out uncomfortable sounds that echoed down the hallway. Residents around him grew uneasy; visitors stared. The charge nurse started to get frustrated.

"Take him out of here," one resident grumbled, loud enough for many to hear.

Janell came up the hallway, noticing the tension. The irritated body language of the seated residents was clear.

She stood next to his wheelchair. Turning his face toward her, she worked to meet his eyes. It was difficult at first, but when their gaze finally locked, his yelling stopped.

"Hi," she said.

Not breaking eye contact, she held his thin, bony, warm hand. Some staff worried he might swing at her, but she assured them she was fine. She hovered close, tracing her finger slowly down his palm.

Once, then twice, like writing a secret only they could read.

He blinked. His mouth moved, but no sound came.

Again, she traced the invisible line, like a lullaby written in touch instead of sound.

His shoulders dropped.

His breathing slowed.

The clenched fist of memory softened in hers.

Silence returned; not heavy, fearful silence, but gentle quiet, something remembered. Maybe a mother. A wife. A daughter. Someone who had once done the same thing, long ago.

Other residents exhaled, unaware they'd been holding their breath.

Janell stayed a few minutes longer, stroking his palm.

No more yelling, just a fragile peace cradled in human touch.

In a nursing home, especially with residents experiencing dementia, touch is more than comfort, it is communication. When words fail, the body remembers. A gentle touch can break through confusion, fear, or agitation in ways language no longer can. Touch is one of the first senses we develop and the last to let go. A stroke on the palm, a handheld, can signal safety, presence, and care. These moments can evoke memories of being soothed as a child, held by a loved one, or a time comforted during illness.

Janell's instinct was to run her finger down his palm.

In a space filled with alarms, noise, and commotion, it's easy to overlook something as simple as human touch.

But sometimes, that's all it takes; a quiet moment, a steady presence, a touch that says, you're still human, and you're not forgotten.

## Chapter 23: Invisible Rod

Janell sat in a hospital bed, staring at the wall with a blank expression. The haze from her painkillers had worn off, and she clutched her chest and shoulder, sitting up straight. Her eyes were fixed on the standard wall clock. She had learned that relief came exactly forty-five minutes after swallowing the pills. Sharp, stinging pain pierced her right breast, shooting to her back. Each movement made her catch her breath.

Too deep, breath felt suffocating.

The sensation was like an invisible rod impaling her breast, driving through her chest and out her back.

Every sudden motion, every cough, every laugh twisted that rod deeper.

### -48 hours earlier-

It had started as a regular weekday morning. In the shower, Janell let the hot water run over her back longer than usual. Soreness still lingered, and she reflected on her restless night. Back pain wasn't uncommon, but tossing and turning had made her question whether it was normal or something more serious. She remembered the discomfort when she turned her neck or shifted to her side. Pillows had been stacked under her neck and shoulders, she discovered the flatter she lay, the sharper the pain.

A strange cramping sensation appeared in her upper abdomen, right beneath her breast. She panicked, thinking briefly about the baby; this could not be what she feared. She considered other possibilities, maybe constipation. She hadn't had a regular bowel movement in days, so she mixed some MiraLAX in her coffee, and within forty-five minutes, relief came.

Dressing for the day, she noticed shortness of breath. Climbing the stairs left her breathless, as if she'd sprinted a short race.

Her intuition screamed that something was wrong.

She drove to the nearest Urgent Care Center and requested vitals. The nurse attending her had a calming presence, the kind of compassion Janell hadn't encountered in a long time. She disclosed that this was her ninth pregnancy, explaining her history of three terminations, three children of her own, and now her third surrogacy journey. The nurse's eyes widened slightly in admiration.

Janell rolled up her sleeve, revealing the tattoo on her forearm: a stork holding a baby, surrounded by dark trees and an orange moon.

"I love this," the nurse said. "The dark trees, the moon—it's beautiful."

"Thank you," Janell replied.

"So, this represents surrogacy, right?" the nurse asked.

"Yes, I guess I would be the stork," Janell said, trying to steady herself as she cupped her right breast.

The nurse's reassurance was steady and warm. She told Janell she had done the right thing coming in, especially since nothing like this had occurred in her other pregnancies.

The doctor arrived and recommended an ambulance transfer to the hospital for a CT scan—a machine the urgent care didn't have. He stressed its importance, and soon Janell was chatting with the paramedic as the ambulance raced through the streets.

At the hospital, her mind spiraled with possibilities.

Was she overreacting? Could this be anxiety, stress, or a panic attack, like so many women were often told?

But she knew her intuition was accurate; she was not overreacting.

The first CT scan was quick. She waited in the ER holding room while blood was drawn and registration completed. She remained cupping her right breast—comfortless comfort, a tether to the pain.

The ER doctor returned, explaining that her D-dimer results were elevated, a test measuring blood clotting. Pregnant women often have higher readings, he said. A CT scan with contrast was necessary to check for a blood clot, though it wasn't always recommended in the first trimester.

Janell hesitated.

The thought of endangering her pregnancy for the scan weighed heavily, but she also needed answers. She thought it best to call the IVF nurse, her care coordinator, at the fertility clinic. Janell was to report any changes in her health to her, so she knew she needed to let her know what was going on. After giving her a quick update, Janell was hoping to get some sort of assurance that she was doing the right thing, being cautious and what not.

When Janell mentioned that the doctor recommended a CT scan with contrast, that was all the IVF nurse was worried about. She didn't have any questions about what Janell was experiencing or her pain level. She began talking to her about her own pregnancy experience and how sometimes her anxiety resulted in pain throughout her body and started saying something about inflammation. Janell understood that she works for the fertility clinic, so her main concern is a healthy pregnancy and baby.

But HELLO!!!

You need a healthy surrogate to have a healthy pregnancy.

Janell felt unheard, her discomfort sidelined. The IVF nurse repeatedly brought up that the CT scan with contrast was not recommended. She could hear the uncertainty in the nurse's voice and realized she needed to trust her own instincts. The urgency of the ER doctor and the throbbing pain in her chest confirmed it.

Her intuition was sharp, and she ended the call.

She agreed to the scan.

The results were immediate: A pulmonary embolism.

Shock, disbelief, and anger collided inside her.

Only seven weeks in, and a blood clot had traveled to her lungs. She followed every IVF instruction meticulously; now she faced a life-threatening complication caused most likely by the estrogen pills. No prior clot history, no family history; nothing to explain why this happened now.

The pain medication finally began to work. Standing, walking, even sitting on the toilet was excruciating. Her body felt weak, her chest heavy, her breath shallow. Moving upright sent lightning bolts from her chest to her back. The simplest motions became monumental tasks.

She would now take blood thinner shots in her stomach twice daily for the rest of her pregnancy—and likely six weeks beyond.

Mentally and physically exhausted, she clutched her throbbing breast with one hand, her stomach with the other. She reflected on her journey; previous pregnancies smooth, no complications, and now this—blood thinners, hospital visits, and a pulmonary embolism.

Her gaze softened as she placed a hand on her abdomen. "Well, little one," she whispered to the baby.

"I guess we're in this together now."

## Chapter 24: Storm of the Flesh

Colette received word that Captain Julien's crew was beginning to pack up. The tide was turning, the cargo loaded; they planned to leave at the end of the week. She rose from her usual post at the market, watching the men prepare the vessel. The captain never showed the slightest interest in her—no lingering glance, no pause in conversation that might hint at more.

Why does it bother me so? she wondered.

His children, the twins.

Over the last few days, she had managed to interact with them somewhat. They were wild and sweet in the way children of the sea often are, with stories of krakens, treasure, and storms shared between mouthfuls of stolen bread. The captain had said little about them, only once murmuring, "They've got their mother's fire. And her stubbornness." He wasn't the warmest father, more a looming figure with rough hands that knew how to steer a ship but not hold a child. The boys adored him anyway, in that fierce, unquestioning way children often do. He had his moments though; Colette watched as he showed them the proper way to tie a knot, joining their tales of mermaids at sea.

The thought of him leaving soon consumed her thoughts more than she liked.

Distorted, unraveling thoughts.

Thoughts of his rejection toward her, of him leaving and taking those sweet boys away—the playful, rambunctious boys who had been two of the brightest sparks her forgotten village had seen in a long while.

It wasn't heartbreak Colette felt; it was something uglier. A heat curling behind her eyes when no one was looking. A fury coiling inside. His lack of interest was insulting. He was so charming with everyone but her, she thought, giving out that crooked, golden smile like coins to beggars everywhere he went. With her, it was always half-words, a quiet nod, a look that never quite landed. He gave the world laughter, but to her, silence.

She thought about the boys, not that she wanted them in her life. It wasn't that; she desperately wanted her own children.

He is a man who can *make* children, she thought.

The boys were proof of that.

Her mind made up on the matter, her racing thoughts consumed her all morning, until she found herself skipping around his ship, humming to herself.

"Hello, beautiful lady, how are you today?" Captain Julien's voice rang from above. His pleasantries were always the same with everyone.

But she wasn't everyone, she thought.

He said hello but didn't seem interested in coming to chat with her.

He was, after all, a man—a man who, she suspected, did not often go without a woman's warmth. But when she thought about it, the whole time he had been ashore, he hadn't shown interest in anyone in the village, unlike his crew mates, who had been indiscreet all over town. No sightings of him with anyone.

What's wrong with this man? she thought.

How dare he come to our village, arrogant. Is no one good enough for him? The more she thought of his pleasant demeanor toward her but without any real sexual advances, the more upset she made herself.

Her thoughts spiraled, distracted only when she overheard the crew talking about a great feast on the ship that night. She knew she needed to appear there.

Colette soon ran into Pascal.

Sweet Pascal.

Tall, perhaps a hand taller than most, his trousers were practical and well-worn, tucked into soft leather boots that had walked a thousand docks without crushing a crab beneath their bottoms. She flirted with him, holding his hand, noticing the strong but delicate fingers and a scar across the back of his hand. Not from battle, he explained, but from shielding a cabin boy from a falling crate during a storm. His eyes, she realized, were sea-glass green, layers of soft jade near the iris fading to misty olive at the edges. Eyes that didn't just look; they listened.

Pascal willingly shared the feast plans and invited her as his personal guest. He was predictable and kind.

He wasn't Julien.

He didn't keep her at a distance or hand out charm like currency meant for others. He enjoyed her company genuinely, asked about the books she read, and walked with the twins when the wind kicked up.

"I've seen a lot of storms, but I've never seen one stand still the way you do," he said quietly.

His words lingered.

No seduction, just quiet truth, placed like a stone on her path. They stayed with her long after they walked away from the market, long after the rage toward Julien had burned out.

The feast had begun before the sun dipped below the horizon. Tables from taverns lashed together with rope, heavy with food. Charred fish dripping with lemon and sea salt, wild boar glazed with honey and burnt oranges, thick spiced stew, crusty bread, fruit, pickled onions, wheels of cheese. Wine poured from barrels as salt-stained sailors crammed shoulder to shoulder, singing songs that grew dirtier with every new bottle of rum.

Colette could never catch Captain Julien alone. He was always surrounded by a crowd. She chased him all night, trying to get his notice. Later that night, she retreated to the back of the ship, away from chaos, leaning her forearms on the railing to watch the moon and stars.

"Beautiful, isn't it?"

A deep voice spoke behind her. Captain Julien.

The moment she stopped searching for him, he came to her.

"The sky? Yes, it's a wonder," she responded.

His conversation flowed easily, his voice calming and sensual when not performing for an audience.

"What is it about the sea you love so much?" Colette asked.

"How much time do you have?" he smirked.

"To ask such a question to a pirate," he replied. His smile was still mesmerizing, though she felt more irritable than ever around him.

She studied his black leather attire, the long coat, the ruby rings, and the black chest hair visible above his shirt.

"You know, you are a stunning man," Colette said. "But I know your secret." She leaned closer, letting him steal a glance down her blouse.

"My secrets? What do you know of them?" he asked.

"I know you're lonely."

"I know loneliness all too well," she added softly, returning her eyes to the sky.

His playful mannerisms halted.

"Beautiful lady, I believe that is the first honest thing I've heard you say."

"Don't call me beautiful," she demanded.

"Why not?"

"You are beautiful," he argued.

Colette turned to him fully.

"Then why don't you fancy me?" she shouted. "Why don't you stare at my body like the others and want to touch me?"

"I'm sure you've seen beautiful women all over the world. How do I compare?"

"Do you always keep your distance ashore?"

"One question at a time," he replied with a smile.

The wind picked up, a strand of her hair blowing across her face. He tucked it behind her ear.

"You are beautiful," he said. "But my heart still aches for another."

"Your children's mother?" she asked.

"Yes. Gabriella." His face filled with pain.

"I haven't been with anyone else since she died. She was my heart. My entire heart."

He quickly shook away the emotion spreading across his face.

"Tell me something real, Colette," he said, changing the subject.

She stared at the stars, then back at his captivating eyes.

"I want a child," she whispered.

"You want to be a mother? That's wonderful. I'm sure you will be one day," he replied, unconvincingly.

Tears pooled in her eyes. She didn't want him to see.

"Why so sad?" he asked.

"I've been with-child twice before, both lost. I only became pregnant twice despite so many frequent attempts. Is my body rejecting a baby? What do you think? In all your travels, you must have heard reasons as to why this happens to women?" Colette looked to the captain for knowledge, for a great wisdom he may have on the topic but was quickly let down by his response.

"Maybe you're just not meant to be a mother in this lifetime," he said without hesitation.

Silence.

The words hung in the air, sharp as salt on an open wound.

Colette's mind reeled. Then, beneath the shock, came a slow, seething current—rage ancient as the sea itself. It rose quietly at first, patient and knowing, as though it had been waiting centuries for those very words.

"How dare you say that to me!" she shouted back at him.

Rage burned within; between his loyalty to his late wife, his rejection towards her, and now this preposterous idea.

He attempted to explain. "I believe we experience many lifetimes, Colette. Perhaps in this one, you're not meant to be a mother. But maybe in another, you will."

She shook her head, furious.

"That is the most ridiculous thing I've ever heard!"

"I will be a mother!"

"You pirate! What do you know?

 Nothing!"


"Colette, please. I wasn't trying to upset you," he said, reaching for her face.


"DON'T TOUCH ME!"

The water under the ship seemed to rumble. Colette's fury was starting to show.

The captain knew it was best not to touch her again. His intuition told him to walk away at that moment, so that is exactly what he did. He motioned for others passing by to leave her alone as well and quickly returned to the feast.


Colette stared at the night sky, trying to steady her breathing, her skin burning, her heart pounding. Her childhood riddles echoed in her mind.

*Die, die, you will cry. Cry, cry, you will die.*


She headed toward the festivities.


I will have every man on this ship if need be. I won't leave until a child is in my belly, she thought, her wrath ignited.

She moved like a siren through the crowd, slowly, deliberately, her fingers sliding beneath her scarf to let her deep orange curls spill free.

Her hair didn't whisper; it roared.

Her eyes scanned the crowd, daring someone to approach.


Louis, a familiar face, was bold enough to ask if she was thirsty. She nodded yes and followed him to the room where they kept the better wines. She tilted the bottle toward her mouth and bit down, pulling the cork out with her teeth. It slid free with dull pop, the scent of ripe fruit and old wood spilling into the air.

She brought the bottle to her mouth and took a long drink.

It burned beautifully.

Hot. Sweet. Sharp.

Panting for air after, she said "I didn't come here to flirt Louis." "I came to feel something burn."

Louis didn't move.

She took one last drink from the bottle and tossed it aside. As she already knew, Louis was a very *giving* man. He was standing there, drunk on the scent of her until she pushed him to sit down on the wooden chair behind him. He looked at her like a sailor facing the storm he thought he could outrun.

"Let me see it, Louis."

"Let me see that beautiful part of you, that you're so proud of."

He obeyed.

His heart hammering, his back in the chair as if held there by ropes.

She circled him. Slow. Silent. Each step measured.

She let the silence stretch. She liked teasing him. Like before.

She placed her hands on his shoulders. He twitched under her touch, not from pain, but from tension, uncertainty, submission. It thrilled her; how much power lived in her stillness.

It *was* beautiful. Hard and throbbing for her.

She lightly stroked it with one finger, like she often does on a person's palm while telling fortunes. She admired it's beauty.

Lifting her long skirt, she straddled him. Letting him ease inside her slowly, they both moaned. The two of them, the same. Still teasing him, she sat still on top of him. He tried to kiss her, but she pulled her face away and grabbed him by the throat. He was so aroused by how aggressive she was being.

He stood up and fucked her, holding her up against the wall. Hard.

He knew she wanted it hard.

She had no interest in his talented kisses or her own pleasure at that moment. She was only focused on getting one thing, his seed.

She pushed him back into the chair again. She grabbed his leather belt and whipped it across his bare chest. The crack of the slap was sharp, and Louis's expression twisted with both pain and a flicker of exhilaration. His body still tingling in pain from the whipping, she sat on his dick again, bouncing fast and wild, grabbing his throat to steady herself.

She rode him hard, too hard.

He attempted to slow her pace but was unsuccessful. He wanted to last longer for her, but she wouldn't allow him. As soon as she knew he came inside her; she pushed him away, the chair tipping backwards with him still in it.

She walked out, and her hunt continued.


The next cabin over she bumped into another man, another pirate with something she needed. She had seen him before in the taverns.

"Tell me my fortune!" he shouted at her, the scent of rum pouring from him.

She smiled and said, "okay." "Follow me." Puzzled for a moment she said yes so quickly; she took him by the hand and said, "come this way." The first empty room they found on the ship, she pulled him into and shut the door behind them.

"Let me see your palm." The drunk man held his hand out. His hands were rough, callused, thick-fingered, the kind of hands made for knotting ropes and breaking a man's nose. Instead of reading the lines, she pressed his hand onto her breast. His face lit up, liking his fortune to come.

"Do you want to fuck me in your future?" she asked.

151

The man nodded, yes, and started to say his name was Bastian. Colette, not listening to him, was in a trance of her own. The words the captain said earlier repeating in her mind.

*"Maybe you're not meant to be a mother in this lifetime."*

She could hear his voice saying it repeatedly in her head. Her clarity unraveling. Her breathing turning into almost a growl.

She looked at the man's scruffy beard in disgust, uneven, streaked with gray. He smelled of smoke and sweat. She did, however, admire the leather necklace he wore with beads and bones, maybe a tooth or two. Some of the bones were bleached white from the sun and sea. Others still carried the faint yellow of age.

"I don't care what your name is, take your pants off." She ordered him.

Bastian, speechless and complaint, tussled to get his trousers off quickly. She pulled him towards her; his weight was nice on top of her. Oddly comforting. Her wetness excited him greatly. A couple strokes in; and she knew it was over. She wiped her inner thighs with her skirt. She grabbed ahold of his necklace that she admired moments before.

"Give this to me." She commanded. She looked at him with an expression that he owed it to her, for his lousy performance. Bastian willingly handed it over. Seconds later, there was a knock on the door. Bastian, yelled "Go Away," at the same time Colette said, "Come in."

Another crewman peeked in. Colette turned over on her belly, her ass in the air. Then. with an arched back like an animal stretching after a long nap, she told the man at the door, to come over to her. Bastian watched as she asked this new stranger his name.

"Who might you be, another pirate to give me what I need?"

I'm Milo, he said.

Milo's face was smooth where others were weathered. His skin still carried traces of softness, the kind that hadn't been burned away by salt and sun just yet. He was lean, almost wiry, like a stray cat, too clever to be caught. He was clearly younger than Bastian.

She reached for him to come over to her.

"I'm a fortune teller Milo."

"Let me see your hand."

In a playful manner she stroked her finger down his palm, following the lines like a map.

Up close, Milo had the prefect pouty lips. Full and perfectly shaped. He wore a face that did not belong on a wanted poster, too delicate, too striking. High cheekbones, a narrow nose.

"Milo, I see a woman in your future."

You do, he started to say, but his sweet pouty lips were calling for her to kiss them. She couldn't resist. Milo tasted sweet, like warm amber and sea salt, with the faintest trace of citrus.

She whispered in Milo's ear, "you taste delicious."

He did. And she kissed him again.

Still holding his palm, she guided his hand between her thighs. She needed more.

His pouty succulent lips tasted like they stole the flavor from some sun-drenched orchard far from here.

Her mind did not stray from her purpose; his lips just happened to be a tasty treat along the way. She whispered again to him, "I need your lips on me, Milo." "I need them everywhere."

She moved his kisses to her collarbone, then to her breast; she watched him as he sucked her nipples. Soft and tender. This young Milo was making her heat rise again. Bastian watched from the corner of the room. She stole another delicious kiss, before whispering in his ear again.

"I need you inside of me."

"Please Milo, I need it."

Milo was hard, Colette could feel that through his trousers. She pulled him on top of her, his kissing, his lips, his tongue, she couldn't get enough. He was deep inside her bliss, her orange curls surrounding them, when the door swung open.

Loud, rowdy crewmembers passing by couldn't help but stop and watch.

Milo tried to pull away, not wanting to be watched by everyone passing by.

"No, Milo, not until you give me what I want!"

Harder, fuck me harder, she moaned out loudly.

Crewmembers cheered him on, wishing they could be in his place. She pulled him in deeper and stole one more sweet tasting kiss. Milo moaned out in pleasure, giving Colette the cum she craved.

Colette quickly got up. Milo's kisses were too sensual. She wanted to stay on track. She was there to get one of these fucking pirates to put a baby in her belly.

She cut through them; they grabbed and tugged at her when she walked by. She walked through the crowd, fixing her hair, trying to hold the cum inside her that was sliding down her legs as she walked. Her long skirt hiding the mess underneath.

She looked for a scruffy, unpleasant pirate. Milo was too pretty, too sensual. Her eyes set on a drunken fool in the back of the crowd. She only had to think of Julien's hurtful words and his smug face to ignite the fire again.

This pirate was dirty, unkept, a ragged scar splitting his cheek from ear to jaw. His nose smashed and crooked, like it's been broken more than bones are supposed to be. She walked towards him, not wasting any time, lowering her blouse to expose her stunning breast. He was clearly drunk and possibly thought he was dreaming.

"Hello." Colette said, standing there in front him.

He had no words, just licked his lips.

Colette grinned and took his hand.

She quickly found another empty cabin.

He fumbled with his buckle on his trousers, his greasy fingers slipping on the rusted metal. Colette felt he was not worth her words or conversation.

She dropped her skirt to the floor and fell to her knees. She placed her palms flat down and waited like an animal to be mounted. His dick was small and worthless at providing any pleasure. To speed things up, she moaned slightly, bouncing back quickly against him. "Right there." "Right there," she said repeatedly. He fucked quick like a rabbit and grunted loudly shortly after. He fell beside her. Shaking his head in dis-belief of how amazing that was, he attempted to speak but then realized she was walking out of the room.

Leaving the room she bumped into Pascal.

She was so happy to see him. Pascal was pleased to see her, as well. He had become a friend over the last couple weeks. The only decent pirate on this entire ship, she thought.

"Pascal I'm sad," she whined to him and pouted her bottom lip.

"Why?" he asked genuinely.

156

"You haven't kissed me since our night with Louis and Margot."

"Do you not fancy me anymore?" She asked, searching for admiration.

"You are the most gorgeous woman I've ever seen Colette, I look for you almost every day." She knew that wasn't the ale talking. Pascal was the only man on this awful ship that seemed to have a heart. Truly.

She knew his words were honest.

"Pascal, meet me in an hour and walk me home, okay?

"Promise me."

He nodded. She left him among the chaos of music and dancing.

Like a predator still hunting, she scanned the crowd—one more, she thought. Her gaze locked onto a new pirate, a fresh target who didn't yet know he was marked. He was strong, broad-shouldered, with long dark hair that framed a face built for trouble. When their eyes met, she tilted her head and gave the slightest gesture toward the water, an unspoken command he seemed powerless to resist.

In a haze, he followed.

The closer she got to the water, the more clothing she took off until she was completely naked. He was under her spell, mesmerized by her beauty under the moonlight. When she entered the water, the sea simmered due to the heat radiating off her skin. The foolish pirate followed her into the sea. The cool waves washed away the sweat, the smell, and the cum of the men before him.

This new man, this new pirate, his arms and chest covered in black tattoo markings from his travels; he grabbed her and kissed her passionately. She removed his clothes completely. Naked in the water, she wrapped her legs around him. He positioned himself to enter her. He was very strong; he effortlessly could hold her up. They grinded against each other, under the moonlight. This man was a superior over.

His strong arms wrapped around her; pressing deep into her; he was the first pirate of the evening to make her cum. Harder, they fucked against each other in the sea water. They barely spoke any words, only heavy breathing, they both came at the same time, both bodies knowing what the other one liked.

When the man attempted to pull out of her, Colette wouldn't let him.

Her hair wrapped around him, wet, like strong vines.

Her Medusa-like eyes started to turn a bright shade of orange.

A magical trance had begun.

Even though the man achieved his climax several times, his dick stayed hard as stone. Colette's body began to shake, she climaxed again and again, every inch of herself pulsating with pleasure.

She used his stone-like dick like a peasant that had one purpose in life, to please her over and over. The man's entire body was exhausted, holding her up, climaxing repeatedly inside her. His body began to tremble in exhaustion. And yet, she didn't let go of her trance.

More…

More… she moaned. "Don't stop," she commanded.

More…Don't stop. More! Don't stop!"

He couldn't stop.

His body wasn't his anymore.

Colette took every bit of semen his body made. Every drop stored inside. She then flew back on top of the water and floated on her back. The man, in pure depletion collapsed into the water.


His body never came back up.


Colette floated there for a minute or two.

Her breathing started to calm. The waves felt in sync with her body.

Her nakedness emerged out of the water, like a victorious warrior walking from a battle.

The fury and fire within had settled.

## Chapter 25: A Kind Goodbye

A comforting Pascal waited on the path home, just as she had asked. "I just wanted to make sure you made it home okay," he said with an easy smile that warmed the chill of the evening.

They walked together until Colette's legs began to falter. She brushed it off with a laugh about too much wine, but Pascal saw through it. Without hesitation, he lifted her into his arms. She let him, feeling for once, cherished instead of chased.

Colette felt like a goddess, being carried all the way home. Pascal warmed water for her bath, lit candles and put clean blankets on her bed. She was impressed by his attentiveness. He made the night even better when he started to message her sore feet. Colette was in a blissful haze of his admiration for her. She adored how he worshipped her.

He sat beside her, his lips finding the back of her neck, while his strong hands rubbed her shoulders. Pascal was patient and caring and caressed her body until she fell asleep.

The next morning, Colette woke to the scent of salt and candle smoke, the morning light spilling across her bed in thin golden ribbons. Pascal beside her, his hair tousled, his breath slow and deep. There was something so gentle about the way he slept. The corners of his mouth were soft, his features unguarded, almost boyish. He looked nothing like the rough-edged men who filled the tavern nights, no shadow of deceit. Just a man who cared too easily.

She turned slightly, studying him, the faint scars near his jaw, the curve of his nose, the way his lashes brushed against his skin. His hand rested open near hers, palm up, as if even in sleep he was offering her something.

For a moment, she let herself believe it was real.

That this warmth, this quiet, could last.

But she knew better.


Colette sat up slowly, pulling the blanket around her shoulders. The small wooden stork on her bedside table caught her eye, delicately carved, its wings half-spread, as if caught between flight and stillness. She ran her fingers over the grain, her throat tightening. It was just like the one Pascal carved for Captain Julien's boy.

He had made it for her while she slept.

Colette was in awe by this sweet gesture.

She smiled when she remembered how kind he was to her last night. She felt she needed to thank him; so naturally, she put her mouth around his sleeping member, to show her appreciation. She began sucking it until it came to life. Pascal stirred, blinking into wakefulness. When he saw her, his smile came easily, unguarded.

"Morning," he said softly, his voice still heavy with dreams. He stretched a long morning stretch, allowing her to devour him. Colette sucked the tip eagerly, twirling her tongue around his throbbing dick. She could tell he was trying hard not to cum. Her own body throbbed with soreness from her sexual escapades from her night before, so she encouraged Pascal to cum in her mouth, letting him know it was okay.

He stopped her.

And paused a bit.


"I love you, Colette." He proclaimed with a trustworthy expression.

Her breath caught.

He looked so certain.

So, trusting.

She could almost see his future without holding his palm— the quiet ache that would live in him if she allowed him to remember her. The hollow that would grow where she once existed.

She brushed his hair back from his face and kissed his forehead. "You are good, Pascal," she said softly. "Better than you know. But you will forget me."

He frowned, confused. "Forget you? How could I?"


"Sweet Pascal."

"Sweet Naive Pascal. You don't love me." She said to him.

"I do love you. I want you to have my child." He proclaimed firmly.

His words, they cut through her....

his words ...

No man has said that to her.

She kissed him, his lips tasted sweet from the wine the night before.

Colette turned on her side, wrapping Pascal's arms around.

She felt safe in his arms. They started pressing against one another as they kissed passionately. He was spooning her from behind, and she moved her body so that he could enter her. He was gentle, he was always gentle.

She did not love him, but he adored her.

She could feel it in the way he held her, the way he kissed her. There was something he was missing in life, and he was finding it within her. She started to really let go at that moment, she let him touch her the way he needed too, she let him love her the way he needed to.

It was beautiful, sensual.

She thrusted back against him.

He smiled every time.

She was getting so wet, which baffled her, she barley found Pascal attractive. His fingers found her clit to rub while he made love to her from behind. His touch was soft, and mindful.

While inside her, she spoke
*"My friend, my friend.*
*How amazing you really are, who knew…*
*But when you leave this cottage, you will forget.*
*Forget everything.*
*Even me. You will forget me too"…*

Her wet blissful magic felt so amazing to him, he wasn't paying any attention to the words she was whispering. She touched his cheek once more, memorizing the kindness there.

Pascal pulled her close to him when he climaxed inside her. He held Colette until she felt it was time for him to let go.

And when he left her cottage that morning, she knew it was for the best.

Chapter 26: Detachment

Janell could already tell how the day was going to go. It was going to be the battle of the sisters. She had one long-term resident who'd lived at the facility for years and a new rehab admit who would probably stay only a couple of weeks before returning home with family.

What did these two residents have in common?

They both had a sister who was going to drive Janell absolutely insane today.

When you're doing your best in a high-stress environment and one family member is constantly complaining, second-guessing, or stirring tension, it can feel exhausting, personal, and deeply frustrating.

Janell's long-term resident had an overly involved sibling who took her "go-to person" responsibility far too seriously. It was one thing to visit often, to be involved in decisions — staff welcomed that. But when it became about control over every detail of a loved one's life, to the point of unhealthy fixation, then they had a problem.

The resident's sister had a camera in the room, as many families did. Cameras could be helpful for both staff and residents. But this sister watched it constantly, as though it were her new favorite Netflix series. Janell knew the look of trouble the second she saw her coming down the hallway. The sister could never just pass her by without reporting something.

"The aides didn't lay my sister down by seven p.m. yesterday; it was closer to seven-thirty. I thought we agreed on seven?"

"I think my sister's roommate is eating her yogurt out of her fridge, again."

"My sister needs to see the dentist. I know she doesn't say her tooth hurts, but I know her facial expressions and she's in pain. She just tells staff she isn't."

"She needs to see the hairdresser Friday; we missed last week because I had her out on pass."

Reasonable requests, sure — but Janell could list a hundred more of them easily. It was as if the sister had to come up with something new every time she saw her.

But today was ridiculous.

The sister came into Janell's office while she was being productive, catching up on much-needed documentation, and demanded her full attention — as usual.

"You will not believe what I caught on my sister's camera today?"

Janell, not overly thrilled to see her, smiled anyway. "What's going on?"

The sister pulled out her phone, her anxiety radiating as she warned Janell, she needed to watch something *"concerning"* about a nurse aide working on her sister's hall.

The video showed the aide in the sister's room. The resident herself wasn't even there. The aide made a small, frustrated gesture at the clothes on the floor, clearly where the resident had pulled them out looking for something to wear. The aide folded several T-shirts quickly and firmly shut the dresser drawer.

"You, see?" the sister asked, eyes wide.

"Umm…I guess I don't see." Janell tilted her head. "What's the problem?"

"She slammed the drawer! She's clearly frustrated with my sister. Do you think she's in a bad mood? Today is my sister's shower day. Should I be worried?"

Janell blinked. "Worried about what?"

The sister spun out a story of what *might* happen. Janell felt her own patience fray. She had paused her charting for this.

"This video is nothing," Janell said carefully. "The nurse aide didn't do or say anything to your sister. Your sister wasn't even in the room. Your concern is that the aide seems irritated?"

Inside, she thought, *"I know the feeling.*

But the sister's anxiety only heightened. She began to list all the other minor grievances about this aide — how she'd moved the sister too close to the TV that morning, how she hadn't brought four coffee creamers, only one, even though she knows she needs more than one.

Janell quieted her voice, speaking to her almost like you would a toddler, assuring her everything was fine and there is nothing to be concerned about.

After lunch, Janell met a new sister.

The brother was a new admit, here for rehab after a hospital stay. His sister had left a demanding voicemail, so Janell called her back.

The sister's voice was sharp and dissatisfied, her brother had signed out earlier, walked next door to the gas station, and bought himself a pack of cigarettes.

Janell explained gently that the facility allowed smoking but that she would retrieve the cigarettes because residents weren't permitted to keep them in their rooms.

"He doesn't need to be smoking at all!" the sister screamed.

She launched into his medical history and reminded Janell that she was his medical power of attorney and didn't want him smoking, period.

Janell replied patiently, "We're a smoking facility. He has the right to smoke. He also has the right to sign himself out and go next door if he wishes. I met your brother yesterday. He's completely cognitive and can make his own decisions. People have the right to make *poor* decisions. Believe me, I wish this building was non-smoking."

Janell continued calmly, "Your medical power of attorney only takes effect when your brother can no longer make decisions for himself. Which he clearly can, even if they're poor decisions about smoking."

"You're the one allowing him to smoke," the sister shrieked. "You're the one killing him!"

Janell bit her tongue. Right — because the forty years he smoked before coming here isn't a factor, right?

The sister then threatened to remove him from rehab. Janell tried to explain, "I'm sure he chose this facility because we're a smoking facility—"

"You're killing him! You're killing him!" the sister screamed. "Go take his cigarettes from him!" she demanded.

Janell assured her she would collect them because it was policy, but that he could still smoke at scheduled times.

"You're killing him!" the sister screamed again.

Janell hung up.

Her patience depleted. She couldn't do it with these sisters anymore today.

That evening, sitting at the dinner table with her kids and husband bickering over who got the last roll, Janell's mind drifted back over her day. She thought about the homeless man who'd cursed her out when she tried to discuss group-home options, the incompetent nurse who had almost given a visitor a shot meant for a resident, the lady who'd worn the same blue-striped T-shirt all week, and whether the aides would finally give her a shower—or just document that she refused again.

She thought about the podiatry referrals she hadn't sent, the signature pages she still needed to fax, the phone call in which a man had told her not to contact him again until his brother was dead. She thought about how many residents were lying in their beds right now, call lights on, needing to go to the bathroom—or just someone to ask if they were okay.

That realization—knowing she couldn't fix everything—could be crushing. She saw people every day who deserved more time, more dignity, more attention than the system allowed. She saw staff burned out, underpaid, overworked.

She saw residents getting mediocre care at best.

Detachment was necessary to keep going, day after day, month after month, year after year. It's easy to find yourself not feeling as deeply. You noticed you nodded and responded, but your heart wasn't in it. You were just going through the motions to get through the day.

It was survival.


Janell had seen suffering in all its forms; confusion, grief, decline, death.

She'd bonded with residents and lost them. She'd heard nonstop complaints, witnessed injustice, and felt powerless to fix it. Emotional overdraft had become her norm.


Detachment, she realized, was her mind's way of saying, I can't keep carrying this all the time. Knowing the realistic side of nursing homes, the side no one likes to talk about—was the hardest part of her job. Tomorrow she'll fix one problem, but countless others she didn't know about would go unreported. Many things she simply could not fix.

It was a conflicting life to live.

Even though she defended the hell out of what she did, she was the first to tell her children

"Under no circumstances do you ever put me in a nursing home."

That night, Janell washed her face and took a melatonin, hoping her brain would shut off. In bed, her throbbing feet pounded from the day. Her body and mind were tired.

As she drifted toward sleep, the words that had haunted her dreams lately floated back again.

*Take three lives and replace them with three…*
*But know this,*
*in which lifetime could it be?*
*Grow three, but not from your family tree,*
*When this happens, you will clearly see…*
She murmured them softly as the darkness claimed her.

# Chapter 27: Womb For Rent

Janell's belly was growing, and the deposits were hitting her account nicely. The soft chime of her phone announced another bank deposit. Most people didn't understand. They thought it was all about the money or that it shouldn't be. But for Janell, it was both. The work gave someone else a dream they couldn't reach alone, and it gave her own family a little breathing room financially.

Her body had become a vessel for nine months. She had given up sushi, soft cheese, her favorite wine. She woke nauseously, fell asleep exhausted. Her feet swelled, her hormones raged. And at the end, she would labor and deliver a child she wouldn't bring home.

It was sacrifice—and sacrifice deserved compensation.

Some people called it exploitation. They pictured poor women being taken advantage of by the wealthy. But that wasn't Janell. She was educated. She had her own children. She read every contract carefully. She had chosen the family. No one was forcing her; she was making this choice.

In choosing this, she helped create families that otherwise couldn't exist. That didn't make it unethical. That made it powerful.

She received a monthly allowance of $300, beginning when the pregnancy was confirmed, meant for gas, healthy food, and prenatal vitamins. When IVF medications began, she received $500, and soon, $800 for maternity clothing—which, as her sixth pregnancy, she could mostly pocket. She was compensated for lost wages from appointments, screenings, embryo transfer day, and other procedures related to the pregnancy. As an experienced surrogate, her base compensation was $70,000. Because she already had medical insurance, the intended parents added $5,000. Payments were divided into ten disbursements, and one of those—$7,500—hit her checking account that morning.

Janell smiled, rubbed her belly, and thought, nice day's work.

A surrogate could gush about loving pregnancy, about helping another family, and that could all be true but yes, the money was a big part, too. In today's economy, trying to save money felt impossible. Large sums hitting her account made possibilities feel possible. Summer camps for her kids, a reliable car, fixing the roof leak, grocery shopping without counting every penny. Security. Freedom.

She was building someone else's miracle and with the compensation, she was slowly building hers. It wasn't selfish or shameful. It was survival, with grace. Twice over: once for the family desperate to grow, once for the family she had already built with love and grit.

Janell understood the concerns.

Surrogacy raised questions about power, autonomy, money, motherhood. People worried about exploitation, commodification, broken bonds. And yes, those things deserved discussion.

She had read horror stories—surrogates pressured to terminate, agencies that didn't protect, contracts full of loopholes.

But at the end of the day, she had chosen this.

She read every line. Asked questions. Set boundaries. Interviewed the intended parents as much as they interviewed her. And still, the critics whispered, "unnatural," "emotionally cold," "doing it for the wrong reasons." But they didn't see the moments that mattered.

No one sees the intended mother's tears when she first heard the heartbeat.

The joy her own children felt on vacations, weekend trips, and the lasting memories they were making because of this work and the money it made.

Janell had learned to let them talk.

Because when she laid her hand on her growing belly, she didn't feel shame. She felt strength.

Let them talk.

She was too busy creating life.

Chime—oh, don't mind that.

That was just another deposit hitting the bank.

Sometimes Janell sneaked away from her desk. She grabbed her laptop and disappeared down the back hallway, past the supply closet and the unused conference room, and found a quiet little spot. She was careful not to make eye contact with anyone who might need something. She knew where she was going. She'd mapped this building like a survivalist; a back living area that very few residents visited, tucked away behind the front door, the lobby, and the constant stream of people popping their heads into her office with something different every few minutes. She found a spot away from the calls, from family members who hadn't visited in months but suddenly wanted updates on bowel movements and therapy goals.

She took a deep breath, knowing at any moment someone might find her. She documented notes from the day—how one resident was refusing showers again, how another was losing weight and showing signs of decline, how no family was listed, just a disconnected phone number. She noted how a discharge meeting had ended with shouting, accusations, and nowhere to go.

Even with all the negative documentation she had to record, this was a nice spot she had found today. No phones ringing, no one tapping on the door. No one asked if she "just had a second," which always turned into twenty minutes of emotional labor. In this hidden corner, she could breathe. She could exist without performing calm, without nodding empathetically while slowly dying inside. She could remember that she was a person, not just a crisis sponge.

She sat for a moment after typing her notes. She closed the chart and powered off the laptop. She observed the room. For once, she didn't rush off to the next task. She looked around—not the office, but at the common room just beyond, where the residents gathered after lunch.

She just watched.

And watched some more.

She started to see them again.

And she remembered; these people were not cases, not "ADLs," not goals in a care plan.

They were stories.

Full, messy, beautiful stories—some nearing the end, some holding on with pure stubbornness.

She watched as one resident gently covered another with a blanket.

And it hit her: she had almost missed this.


In the rush, in the burnout, in the endless, breathless pace of paperwork and panic, she had almost stopped seeing the charm, the tiny details that used to fill her up.

Sometimes she just needed to slow down. To observe.

To just be here in this strange little world of fading memories and quiet kindness.

Janell noticed one resident humming softly as she folded a sweater on her lap, her fingers moving carefully over the fabric. Another resident, who rarely spoke, watched her with a small, approving smile, nodding slightly as if sharing a quiet joke no one else could understand. Across the room, a man shuffled his chess pieces with deliberate slowness, entirely absorbed, while a young aide knelt beside him, patiently explaining a move he didn't quite grasp.

In that moment, Janell saw a subtle rhythm, a quiet interconnection—the little ways they cared for one another, even when the world outside this room demanded nothing but rules and schedules.

For once, the chaos of her day melted into the background, and she could simply witness the human tenderness blooming here-softly kept, unnoticed and unhurried.

In that small moment, it felt like the world had exhaled. Everything sharpened. The soft voices, the easy laughter, the way people cared for one another without thinking. Janell realized how rare it was to witness something so simple and so good, untouched by hurry and demand.

And for the first time that day, she felt herself soften too, as if this quiet kindness had reached out and steadied her.

Chapter 29: The Weight of Waiting

Janell adjusted her laptop on the kitchen counter, feeling the familiar weight of the baby growing inside her. She rested a hand lightly on her belly, letting the small shifts and kicks remind her that life was moving inside her, even before the world fully knew it. She took a slow breath, feeling, in the quiet of the morning, the subtle weight of waiting pressing gently on her chest—the anticipation, the hope, the responsibility she carried across oceans and time. Soon, the family on the other side of the call would fill her screen with faces she had never seen in person yet already knew in a way that went beyond words.

The video call connected, and the faces of the family appeared, framed by the soft light of their living room thousands of miles away. Their expressions carried all the weight of hope, worry, and something she could not quite name; a longing that mirrored her own, though in a different way.

"How are you feeling today?" the mother asked, her voice soft, careful, full of hope.

Janell's hand rested lightly on her belly as she answered, describing the baby's kicks, her own energy, and the weekly checkups.

But as she spoke, a quiet shiver ran through her—an instinct, a flutter at the edge of her consciousness that had nothing to do with nerves. She imagined the child's life ahead, fleeting glimpses of joy and challenge, and she felt, in a way no ultrasound could measure, the threads of connection between them already forming.

The parents' questions continued—what she had eaten, how she was sleeping, whether she had felt any unusual movement. Janell answered each one carefully, aware of how much their worry and hope relied on her, yet she also allowed herself a private moment of reflection. Carrying this child connected her to something larger, something beyond the routine and paperwork of her other life. She thought of the residents at the nursing home, of their stories, of how she had learned to witness life fully even when they were constrained by walls and schedules. Here, too, she was witnessing life, but this one had not yet taken its first breath.

The call lingered, and for a few moments, she allowed herself to simply observe the family, the way their eyes softened when they looked at her, the way their voices carried careful optimism. She spoke of the baby's kicks, of the moments when she laughed at her own clumsiness or sighed at her own tiredness, of the ways pregnancy reshaped every ordinary day into something extraordinary. And all the while, she felt a subtle pulse of connection—threads weaving silently across continents, binding her, the child, and the family in a quiet tapestry of hope.

When the call finally ended, Janell remained still, her hand resting lightly on her belly. She let the silence settle around her, feeling the baby shift, a gentle reminder of life's persistence, its insistence on continuing no matter the distance or circumstance. For a moment, she closed her eyes, letting the images of the family linger in her mind, imagining the life that awaited them and the role she played in bringing it into being. She understood, as she often did, that she was both observer and participant, witness and protector, keeper of a story that was already beginning even before the first cry.

Janell exhaled slowly, a smile touching her lips. In this quiet kitchen, far from the chaos of her other work, she felt the familiar pulse of something larger. The world outside might never see the quiet miracles that happened here, but she did. And for now, that was enough. She rested her hand over her belly and felt the full, profound weight of waiting, knowing that patience, hope, and connection were as vital as life itself.

## Chapter 30: The Bond Beneath the Water

Janell sat in her recliner, feet propped up, noticing her swollen ankles. She scrolled through the endless options Netflix offered but found nothing worth watching. Frustrated, she turned the TV off. Slowly, she caressed her round belly, her fingers tracing the faint stretch marks like memories etched in skin.

The baby was a boy.

Ultrasound appointments had always been special days; the fluttering heartbeat, tiny fists and feet, the unmistakable proof that she was carrying someone's son.

A boy she would never raise, for a family halfway across the world.

She recognized the mood pressing down on her. It was the last time she would carry a baby. The last time she would feel life flutter beneath her skin. The last time she would fall asleep with one hand on her stomach and wake to small nudges, reminders that she was not alone.

It was her third surrogacy journey.

She knew the process, the part she played, the inevitable goodbyes. But today, everything felt slower. Softer.

"This is it," she whispered. "The last one."

And suddenly, she didn't know if she felt relief or grief. Not because she wanted another child of her own, she didn't. But because this part of her, this ability to create and carry life for someone else, was almost over.

"Will you ever know me?" she whispered.

The little boy she would never raise yet somehow felt so connected to. Her hand rubbed in small circles over her belly, trying to memorize the shape of him before time ran out—the way he stretched, the way he settled when she hummed. The rhythm they had built together, just the two of them.

She wondered who he would become. Would he grow up in a home filled with books and lullabies, or loud dinners and busy mornings? Would he love dinosaurs or space? Be cautious or wild at heart?

Would he feel a pull, sometimes, to something he couldn't explain?

Would he ever sense her—not as a face, not as a name, but as a softness inside him? A calm that steadied him when life grew too loud.

Would they tell him about her?

Would they say she rubbed her belly every night and whispered, you are loved.

Would he know that she cried, not from regret, but from the strange ache of loving someone she was destined to let go of?

She pressed her palm a little firmer against the curve of her stomach. Maybe he would never know the love she held for him in the quiet hours when no one was looking. Maybe he would never know the sacrifices, the physical ones, the emotional ones. The nights she couldn't sleep, torn between detachment and overwhelming connection. Maybe he would never know that she loved him in a different kind of way; a fierce, protective love that carried him safely through months of storms and stillness, of cravings and chaos, of joy and isolation. And maybe he would never know the scars she would carry—not just the faint ones etched into her skin, but the invisible ones.

Maybe he would never know any of this.
But still, she loved him.

The emotions rose, heavy and unrelenting. She decided to run herself a bath. The house had finally fallen quiet. Dishes rinsed, counters wiped down, she stood at the threshold of the bathroom, one hand supporting her back, the other resting on the curve of her belly. Her body ached; her hips felt wide, and her ankles puffed like rising dough.

She turned on the faucet. Warm water gushed into the tub, steam fogging the mirror. Under the sink, mismatched Bath & Body Works candles waited, Vanilla Bean Noel, Midnight Amber Glow, and a half-burned Eucalyptus Rain.

The chaotic scents were oddly comforting.

The tub filled slowly. She lowered herself in, awkward and deliberate. Her belly floated at the surface like a moon. She sank deeper and let the day melt away. Somewhere between Vanilla Bean and Eucalyptus, she found peace. The water went still. Half-submerged, hand cradling her belly, steam rising in lazy swirls, the only sound was the soft ripple when she shifted slightly.

She closed her eyes.

Warmth consumed her—not from the water, but from deep inside.

When she opened her eyes, she noticed the water around her stomach had changed. A soft orange light bloomed beneath the surface, like the glow of a sunset trapped in the bath. It simmered gently, rich and deep like amber stirred into water.

It didn't feel like her bathroom anymore.

It felt like a temple.

A place between worlds.

At first, she thought it must be a reflection, water catching the candlelight. But when she lifted her belly just enough, the glow followed. It pulsed gently, like a heartbeat, slow and steady. She held her breath, placing both hands over the curve. The glow brightened beneath her palms, and she felt something—not a kick or flutter, but a small, deliberate press.

It was him.

Tears slid from the corners of her eyes into the bath. She leaned back, half-floating, letting her hands glide over her belly. The baby stayed still. The glow dimmed. Or perhaps it had never been there at all.

Whatever had just happened—real or imagined—carved something into her, quietly and permanently.
Everything disappeared, stress, aches, worries, timelines.

There was only this.
Only her.
The water.
And the baby.

## Chapter 31: Tides of Tears

The day started pleasantly, Colette stayed home all day. She needed a day to herself. She sat cross-legged in her armchair, a half-read book resting on her lap, its pages fluttering in the light breeze that slipped through the open window. She sat the book aside and wandered barefoot outside where she spent many hours nurturing her small garden. She hummed a pretty tune to herself while she painted different vases and bowls outside, the scent of lavender in the air, her washed linen drying in the sunshine. At one point she became distracted and followed a butterfly. She watched as it landed on different flowers and trees in her yard until it disappeared into the wooded forest. She pulled a few weeds, plucked a ripe tomato and gathered some wildflowers to take inside. The act of caring for living things, without urgency, was its own kind of prayer.

Theo's wife brought over some rosemary butter, which Colette mixed with some chicken and potatoes and had it simmering all afternoon. The kettle, old but loyal, hummed as it heated water. When the evening hours approached, she built a small fire in her chimney to get the chill out of her house. She had been wearing her floor length white night gown for most of the day, now that it was cooler, she covered her shoulders with an old comfy shawl. Colette sat at her quaint circle table, she admired the red vase she painted, that now had a mixture of sunflowers and wildflowers coming out of it.

The quiet was nice.

Peaceful.

In these moments of serenity, it was hard not to daydream. She thought of the sound of pitter-patter feet running around, and laughter in the air. She longed to make playful drawings on the walls with her small children one day. She had thoughts about dancing in the kitchen and cooking for more than just herself. It all sounded so splendid. After being lost in thought for a while, she then indulged in supper and some red wine. Eating slowly, savoring every bite. When her tummy was nice and full, Colette locked her windows and blew out most of the candles that were scattered around. She yearned to crawl under her quilt and drift off into the wonderland of dreams. Her bed was calling her name.

A loud knock shattered the stillness.

Colette flinched, the peaceful rhythm of her day scattering like birds from branches.

She was not expecting company, nor did she want any.

Another knock. Firmer. Impatient.

She rose, slowly, wrapping her shawl tighter around her shoulders as she moved to the door.

"Who is it?" she called out to the door.

"It's Captain Julien, beautiful lady, may I have a word?"

Colette cracked the door just a little, "good evening, captain", she whispered standing in the doorway.

"I must have a quick word with you," he said as he pushed the door open fully in a very domineering way, not waiting for an invitation.

Her tranquil cottage just moments before, was now being infringed on by his loud presence. She attempted to ask if he wanted some tea, but he jumped into conversation rather quickly.

"Colette, my ship returns to the sea in the morning, and I just hated how our conversation ended the last time we spoke." His charming words started to flow, as he told her "I wanted to see your beautiful face once more, before I left."

"Really?" she questioned him.

"You are always surrounded by many faces, I didn't know you thought of mine."

"And now, the night before you leave, I find you here at such a late hour."

"Yes, here," he said as he looked around her tiny cottage, as if it was not up to his standards. He roamed around, wearing his tall black boots with a buckle on the side that made a clacking noise as he walked,

"Before you got upset the other night, we had very nice conversation, don't you think?

"You have a way with people, Colette."

"I shared things with you, I spoke of my Gabriella and my feelings, I don't normally do that."

Colette sat at her small round table, moving the vase around as if it were in the wrong spot, watching him inspect all the nick knacks around her home.

"Colette this next journey of ours, it is going to be a long one, I may never make it back to this little village of yours".

"Life of a pirate, I suppose," Colette said nonchalantly.

She no longer yearned for the captain like she did when he first arrived.

At this moment, the only thing she yearned for was her bed, her quilt, her pillow and her dreams.

Why is he here, what does he want, she thought.

As she sat in her wooden chair, he stood next to her, towering over her. He pulled at the string at the top of her night gown in hopes it would unravel. Slowly he pulled at it again, intentionally rubbing her nipple with his thumb through her nightgown.

"I'm going to be gone at sea for a very a long time"….He said again.

Colette was in no mood, she had been trying to seduce him for weeks, and she hated to be ignored. She pulled her shoulder back, she was also quite bothered that he interrupted her blissful, perfectly content evening.

"Julien look," she started to say

"Captain," he interrupted.

"You can address me, as Captain," he firmly said, standing tall as if he was commanding orders to his crew.

Colette rolled her eyes as she stood up from the chair, her face close to his. The smell of rum poured from him; she twirled her finger around one of his long braids and said,

"*Captain* Julien." Emphasizing the word captain.

"You have had weeks to get to know me, why now?

"Why the night before you leave?

Now standing face to face, her tongue slid across his bottom lip, when she finished her question.

He pressed his hand to her pussy, grabbing it, on the outside of her nightgown. His touch was not at all soft or gentle; nothing like the pirate that was in her home the day before.

Answering her question sharply, he said "Guess I want to find out, what the fuss is all about."

Normally, having a good-looking man, a pirate at that, alone with her, in the evening hours of her home would be enticing, but she couldn't shake the eerie feeling in the room. He attempted to unravel the top part of her nightgown, again.

She pulled away, again.

He laughed, as if she was teasing him on purpose.

His frustration showed and his tone raised., "I don't understand women like you"

"You have been prancing around, half naked for weeks, trying to get my attention, and now you have it. My men tell me you do fortune telling for the travelers who come and go through this village."

"Yes, I do."

"Here lately I've been helping people too, my predictions have been fruitful and uplifting"

"Helping them?" The captain smirked.

"You think you're helping them, huh?" His laughter started to become theatrical.

Colette didn't like the way he was speaking to her. In her attempts to take control of the moment, she said, "Let me read your fortune."

"Simple girl, your trickery will not impress me." His words rolling off his tongue with insults and arrogance.

She took a hold of the captain's hand, rubbing his wrist and forearm while getting him to sit across the table from her. She took her middle finger and stroked it up a down his palm. He appeared frustrated, he clearly thought fortune telling was nonsense.

"You have a dark past" Colette started to say.

"I thought fortune tellers told the future, not the past," he said, rudely.

Colette continued, "Sometimes we need to revisit the past to know where we are headed."

"Sounds like gypsy nonsense to me," he mumbled.

Colette continued, "You have experienced loss."

A frustrated Captain then said, "yes."

 "I already told you my wife, Gabriella passed away."

"But You have lost others, haven't you?" Colette still stroking his palm, her eyes raising to meet his.

"Your brother" …she paused…

"Your father" …"

"Oh dear, a close friend in a dreadful way."

"Enough Witch!" he slammed his hand down on the table.

Colette jumped back, he came towards her with darkness in his eyes, and he shouted,

"What do you know?"

"Simple girl."

"You know nothing!"

"This nothing of a town you live in," he laughed slightly to himself.

"You think you're helping people?"

"Ha, the only people you help are the men that need a quick fuck!"

Colette darted for the door but was intercepted. His strong body blocked her like a stone wall. He grabbed her face, "Simple girl, you are a whore."

My crew mates, you left them wonder-struck apparently,

"Earth shattering" one man even said.

"Are you? Are you as amazing as they say Colette?"

He pushed her up against the wall.

"Julien Stop!" She pushed his arms back and shouted at him,

"So, this is the real pirate, right?"

"The great captain everyone seems to love"

"With your tales of great adventures, whatever, I see you. The real you."

They scuffled against one another until they were down to the floor.

Julien held her down and yelled next to her ear,

"You want a baby so bad right?

"That's what you want, right!"

He was fighting to get in between her legs, trying to pull her knees apart; Colette found strength in her legs she didn't know she possessed as she kicked him back and shouted,

"Not from you!"

His laughter was sinister; he clearly was turned on by her fighting against him. He was strong, like a bear pinning down a deer. There was no chance of her getting him off her, he was so strong. He tried at first to take off her undergarments, but since she wouldn't stay still, he just pulled them to the side so he could enter her. Once inside, he let out a loud holler, as if he wanted the world to know he made contact inside.

Colette remembered what he had mentioned before. What he said about not being with anyone since his wife passed. I'm sure he won't last long; her inner voice told her. She attempted to find comfort in that thought. To hopefully speed up the process, she stopped resisting.

She attempted to kiss him, but he pushed her face away. He was cold, and barbarous in his touch. She wrapped her legs around him, trying to convince herself she was enjoying it, trying to convince him. He started saying awful things to her. With his lips by her ear, his mouth smelt of rum, his breath gamy.

"Simple whore."

"A whore and a pirate, you and I are the same"

"I find one like you at every port I stop at."

"Someone, no one will miss."

She listened to his vulgar words, hoping that if she moaned just right and played along, it would make him finish quickly and all this would be over. It was one strong stroke after another, deep inside her. For a mere moment, she caught herself enjoying it.

"What's wrong with me?" she thought.

She didn't want him, she didn't want this, but she felt her body taking it, she felt herself succumbing to him. She was furious at herself for enjoying it. Right there on her small cottage floor, on her favorite woven rug. They moaned together, fucking as if they hated one another.

She did hate him.

She wouldn't allow herself to cum, she did not want him to have that satisfaction, on top of everything else. But what happened next caught her by surprise. The way he was breathing, the way he was moaning, she knew he was about to finish, but instead he pulled out of her, and quickly stood up.

He paced back and forth quickly. Colette was puzzled as to what was going on, she knew he hadn't finished yet. He was mumbling underneath his breath; she could not make out what he was saying to himself. She sat up and reached for him to come to her.

"My Captain, tell what you like."

"What pleases you?"...

Seconds after she asked the question, he stood over her, she soon felt the sting of the back of his hand slapping her face to the ground. There was a ringing in her ears, and for a few seconds she couldn't see.

Her cheek throbbing, his ruby stone rings felt like rocks against her face.

He pulled both arms behind her back; her face burrowed into her favorite woven rug. He plunged himself back inside her, thrusting a few more hard pumps and pulled it out again. He paced beside her once more.

She had rough sex before, that is not what this was…

Her tears started to make a wet imprint on her rug. He grabbed a fist full of orange curls, bringing her face up off the ground slightly.

He mocked her for crying.

"Simple girl, are you crying?"

"I'm not hurting you, am I?"

"You were enjoying it, I could tell," He whispered beside her, before throwing her head down to the ground completely.

"Poor simple girl is this not what you wanted?" he shouted has he paced beside her.

"Throwing your cunt to everyone that will take it! Teasing and toying with my men!"


On the ground, trembling, feeling defeated; Colette knew she was not strong enough to fight him off. She knew no matter how loud she yelled; no one was within ear's reach. She knew this wicked man would continue until she was dead. She knew this is why he waited to see her until the night before they set sail.

How many women has he done this too? she thought.

Not knowing what else to do; Colette's back now flat on the ground, she raised up her knees, her ankles together; and then let her legs fall to the side.

Her pussy lay barre, open and exposed.

He paced beside her, telling her he didn't want that disgusting cunt. Holding his cock in his hand, he stroked it as he spoke to her,

"How many men have you had?" He questioned with a look of judgment and hatefulness.

"How many men have you bewitched with that disgusting thing?"

Colette panting on the floor, like a wounded animal. He circled around her, never taking his eyes off her. He licked his lips like a wolf about to finish it's meal.

He slowly crouched down to the floor with her, the slower he moved, the more she trembled. She could feel his breath on her inner thighs. So worried he would strike her again, she jumped when he began to lick her clit. His tongue was slow at first. He seemed to want to savor her taste. Then his tongue began to go faster. She squirmed on the floor trying not to enjoy it. Trying to inch away, but he grabbed her hips and dove his face into her. She couldn't help but thrust back, pressing her clit hard against his tongue. She wanted to cum; her body was tingling. With a quick consistent motion, she pressed her clit harder against his tongue, his thumb entering her ass, making the sensation of it all even better.

He stopped.

She heard the sinister laugh again.

For a moment she thought, "Is it over?

Maybe that's all he wanted to do. Tease me, teach me a lesson.

He spat in his hand and stroked his dick.

Then he spit on her.

He spit on her exposed body that laid open for him.

"Disgusting cunt" he said, looking into her eyes as if she was everyone he ever hated.


This time, he didn't stand back up to return to his pacing, He crawled back on top of her; his dick plunging back inside of her. His hand now around her throat. He drove into her with a punishing, furious rhythm, each thrust fueled by something darker than desire.

His anger bleeding into every motion, each stroke harsher than the last.

He was fury made flesh, primal and terrifying.

His grip around her throat was getting tighter. She started to lose consciousness, the edges of her vision darkening as his grip held her captive. With her eyes completely shut now, she started to see an orange glow. She felt as if her mind was detaching from her body.

Her lips barley parted, she whispered,

"Gabriella"

The captain was caught off guard. His pounding came to a halt; still inside her, he raised up to look at her.

Colette opened her eyes and found a look of terror on the captain's face.

They were no longer surrounded by Colette's orange curls. Captain Julien had his hand around a women's throat that now had long wavy black hair.

"Gabriella?" he gasped.

It was no longer Colette's' face that was red, no longer Collette's lip that was bleeding.

The woman, now in his hands, her head fell to the side.

His eyes searched for the mole.

The mole on Gabriella's left cheek. The mole he kissed so many times before they fell asleep next to one another. When his eyes found it. His hands let go quickly, and he pulled them back.

The woman's eyes fluttering to open fully.

"Ju Ju," she whispers to him, her arms reaching for him completely.

His breathing quickly elevated from fear and bafflement.

He started pulling away,

No, no, no….

No no no no, this can't be, I don't understand.

"Ju Ju we don't have much time, only mere moments before I'm gone again."

"Don't think, just feel me," she instructed.

Her familiar embrace drew him closer to her. Teardrops formed at both eyes, still shaking in terror, he said "Gabriella, it's really you"

His arms wrapped around her, holding her close to his chest.

Close to his heart, as if he was putting a piece back in that had fallen out.

He kissed her red cheek; he kissed her sweet mole.

"The witch Julien, she is allowing me to be here with you, but for only mere moments."

"Please, don't let go. Please Ju Ju"

She pulled him completely on top of her. Kissing him passionately. He felt weak and collapsed next to her. His mind was trying to make sense of it all. confused, but only she kissed him that way. He surrendered, believing this had to be real.

His touch became soft and considerate.

His tears pouring out, as he kissed his dear lost love, Gabriella. Their familiar bodies falling into one another as they always did.

She whispered in his ear, "Ju Ju I love you."

Hearing her words, her familiar voice; he began to sob even more.


Now.

 In Collette's voice, he heard


*"Cry Cry, you will die*
*Die Die, you will cry."*


"Poor simple pirate."

"Are you crying?"

He flew himself back and away from her, Gabriella was gone.

Colette stood up, her words clear and direct.

"You mocked my tears, Simple Pirate!"

"You will know tears from this night on."


*"The waves in the Ocean are many, not shy...*

*Every time the water splashes on your ship,*

*Cry Cry Cry"*


*"The waves in the Ocean are many, not shy...*

*Every time the water splashes on your ship,*

*Cry Cry Cry"*


Captain Julien, panicked with fear, panicked with embarrassment and terror, he grabbed his

clothing, his half-covered body ran out the yellow door and into the night.


He heard Colette's words start to fade the further he ran.


*"The waves in the Ocean are many, not shy...*

*Every time the water splashes on your ship,*

*Cry Cry Cry"* ...

*"The waves in the Ocean are many, not shy...*
*Every time the water splashes on your ship,*
*Cry Cry Cry"*

Chapter 32: Threads of Care

Janell often observed her residents sitting in the dining hall or staring out a window, wondering what their thoughts consisted of. Some didn't know the year, month, or even the day of the week, but remembered bits and pieces of their childhood. One lady, in her nineties, had asked today, "I'm looking for my mother. Did you see her walk past here?"

Another woman walked by with her purse. Janell asked, "Where are you going?"

"I must go; I need to pick up the kids," the resident replied. Knowing her children were grown adults with families of their own, Janell smiled and said, "Okay, don't be late."

Being a social worker in a nursing home required a very specific kind of personality, one that blended emotional resilience with deep compassion. It wasn't just a job; it was a daily act of showing up for people in the last chapter of their lives, often when they were most vulnerable and forgotten. Janell knew she couldn't do this work without a soft heart and a thick skin. Thick enough to take the yelling from a daughter who hadn't visited in six months. Thick enough to handle the death paperwork while thinking about the next best option for the current room. But soft enough to remember which resident loved lemon drops. Soft enough to sit by a dying man's side because no one else was coming. Soft enough to let a woman with dementia hold her hand like she was her daughter, to ease her mind a little.

The social worker role was complicated. Janell was often the rule enforcer. Residents saw her as the one who took things away—freedom, cigarettes, car keys, even independence at times. They didn't always like her; she understood that. She was the one who said no more than yes.

"No, you can't go outside alone."

"No, you can't drive anymore, and your car is not parked outside."

"No, you can't keep a bottle of vodka in your nightstand."

She was the one who took things away, even when she didn't want to. Sometimes, they looked at her like she was the warden, like she was the enemy. But what they didn't see was what she carried home—the guilt, the questions.

Did she do the right thing? Did she protect them? Or did she just chip away at what little freedom they had left? She didn't always know. All she knew was that she cared. Even when they glared at her, cursed her under their breath, or she felt like the villain in someone else's final chapter, she would still come back tomorrow and try again to have a better day.

Social workers choose this profession because they wanted, or needed, to do something meaningful in their lives. Janell strove to improve the lives and wellbeing of a vulnerable population. In the nursing home, her voice was the resident's voice. She stood up for their rights, advocated for their wants and needs, and in doing so, got to know their behaviors, who they were today, and possibly a glimpse of who they had been.

Janell had worked in this setting long enough to know the rhythms of the place better than the back of her own hand. She knew when the hallways hummed with morning routine and when they fell into afternoon hush. She knew which resident was about to have a meltdown before they even furrowed their brow. She knew exactly which resident would be agitated every Wednesday afternoon, always after his daughter visited. He didn't say much, but she saw the clenched jaw and the way he twisted his wedding ring. She usually sat with him afterward in the courtyard, talking nonsense until the tightness in his shoulders let go.

It was a strange gift, this knowing—knowing what they needed before they knew how to ask. She knew when the weather would make joints stiff and moods sour. She knew when family visits would cause more harm than good. She knew which residents needed extra pudding cups, and which just needed to be heard.

Sometimes, she must have looked like she wasn't doing much—just wandering the halls, sipping coffee, making small talk—but in reality, she was holding the threads together, making sure the fabric of this place didn't unravel. There was no manual for how to read a person's silence or the meaning behind a closed curtain, but Janell had learned, over years and years, to read them all. Now, without needing a chart or a care plan, she just knew.

It wasn't magic.

It was love wrapped in repetition.

Janell walked past a room that caught her attention. A resident who rarely ever sat up in bed was now upright, staring out the window, muttering under her breath. Curious, Janell stepped closer, studying the woman she barely knew. Her skin was wrinkled, her body frail, bones protruding beneath pale, thin flesh. She rocked slightly back and forth, whispering urgently.

"The child, the child, please, someone, get the child, she can't see. She went into the water."

"The child, the child, please, someone, get the child, she can't see. She went into the water."

Janell approached slowly, keeping her voice calm and steady. "Ma'am, there's no child. I'm sure your children are grown. You're safe here, can I help get you anything?"

The woman's eyes darted around the room, her hands squeezing the thin blanket across her lap. Her voice wavered, torn between fear and confusion, a jumble of memories and delusions tangled in the fog of dementia.

The elderly lady turned to Janell, her eyes falling on the very large, pregnant belly beneath Janell's sweater. Her expression shifted, a flicker of recognition, or something deeper, passing across her face. Slowly, she reached out, her frail hand hovering for a moment before lightly resting on Janell's belly, trembling with the effort.

The elderly lady's gaze fixed on Janell, and in a low, trembling voice, she said,

"It's almost time."

Janell assumed she meant the baby—that the woman thought she was close to giving birth, but something about the tone made her pause. It felt as if the words carried a meaning beyond the obvious, something ancient and unknowable. A quiet, eerie weight settled over the room, filling the space between them with a strange, silent awareness.

Janell gave the elderly lady a gentle smile and squeezed her hand lightly. "I'll see you tomorrow, ma'am," she said softly, though the woman's cryptic words still echoed in her mind.

With a final glance at the frail figure in the bed, Janell turned and left the room, her steps slow as she made her way back to her office.

While getting in her car to go home for the day, the evening air felt ordinary, almost mundane but in the back of her mind, the weight of the woman's words lingered,

"It's almost time."

# Chapter 33: Arms Around her Belly

Janell moved slowly down the produce aisle, pushing her cart, her mind wandering over recent Pinterest recipes as she eyed a stack of overripe bananas. A woman beside her offered a polite smile.

"Oh, you're just glowing," the woman said warmly. "When are you due?"

"About four weeks to go," Janell replied.

"Is the nursery ready?"

Janell shook her head. "I'm not sure. It's not my baby—I'm a surrogate."

The woman blinked, pausing mid-reach for a bag of apples. "Oh," she said. "Wow, that's… interesting."

There was a brief, uncomfortable silence.

Janell had heard every reaction imaginable during her surrogacy journeys, curiosity, subtle judgment, awkward questions.

"I don't know how you could do that," the woman finally said. "Carry a baby for nine months and just hand it over. I know I couldn't do that."

"The parents have been through a lot to get here," Janell said evenly. "I'm just helping them grow their family."

The woman offered a tight-lipped smile but didn't argue further. "Still, I don't think I could ever give away a child like that."

Janell met her gaze steadily. Well, I'm not giving away my child, she said. I'm giving someone else their child. There's a big difference.

The woman turned away without another word. Janell reminded herself that not everyone would understand and that was okay. Her reasons lived inside her heart, and in the hopeful hands of the parents waiting to meet the little life she carried. Some days would be harder than others, but she never regretted choosing to be a part of something bigger than judgment.

She climbed into her car, hands resting on the steering wheel, and unexpectedly laughed. The encounter stung briefly, but it didn't linger. She glanced down at her belly, feeling the slow shifting of life beneath her skin.

This baby, someone else's baby, would have a story that began with love—not just from the parents, but from Janell too. From her choice, her sacrifice, her strength. That stranger in the store would never understand what it was like to carry something that wasn't hers and still love it with the kind of love that lets go. That took courage. That took power most people couldn't imagine.

The rain felt heavy and loud that night, pressing against the windows and blurring the world outside. Thirty-five weeks. The countdown had shifted from abstract to real. The baby was ready, but Janell wondered if she was. For the first time in a long while, she didn't feel strong. She felt hollow. The closer she got to the finish line, the more undone she became.

The baby shifted inside her, stretching, and she gasped. "We're almost there, little one," she whispered.

And then she cried.

Not the soft tears she had allowed herself before, the ones that slid quietly down her cheeks, but full, chest-shaking sobs. She wept for the closeness that was about to end. For the quiet hours where she had been the baby's whole world. For the ache she hadn't wanted to admit—she was going to miss this.

Her daughter entered the room, face puzzled. "Why are you crying?"

Janell brushed back her daughter's ponytail. "I'm not sad because something is wrong," she explained. "I'm sad because something big is almost over. And sometimes, saying goodbye is hard."

Her daughter wrapped her small arms around Janell's belly, instinctively protecting the life inside her, and grounding Janell herself.

The sight steadied her.

Even amidst her sadness, this moment—the warmth, the trust, the steady presence of her child—lifted her. It didn't erase the pain, but it reminded her why she was on this journey.

She held her daughter tighter.

This child, *her* child, reminded Janell of the love she had known and why she gave this gift to others. She could feel the grief and still feel the joy. She could mourn the closeness she would soon lose and celebrate the love that remained.

Janell was mother.

A giver.

A woman making space for another family's joy while holding tight to her own.

# Chapter 34: The Glow Within

The nausea came like a wave, sharp and certain. Colette leaned against a tree, eyes fluttering shut, pressing her hand to her belly, not out of discomfort, but out of possibility. And then, she smiled.

It was exactly how it had begun the last two times. The smell of roasting duck, the familiar betrayal of her senses. The nausea passed quickly, but the knowing stayed. She became aware that she was less interested in a man's touch. And just like before, there was now soreness in her chest; she enjoyed the discomfort, for she knew what it meant. Her dreams grew more vivid than usual, and the sudden craving for sour plums, picked too early from the tree behind her cottage, tugged at her senses. Every symptom was a bell ringing softly inside her. Each whisper said, life is here again.

She had longed to be a mother for as long as she could remember, not out of some romantic notion, not to fix anything broken. The desire lived in her marrow, always there, to raise another soul with stories, songs, and strong roots. The villagers never understood her longing. Women were meant to wait, to marry, to follow the rules. But Colette was never made for their order. She chose her own rhythm.

It did not matter which sea-blooded stranger left a piece of himself behind. She had no way of knowing which pirate had fathered the child, and she didn't care. That was what she told herself. And mostly, it was true. The sea had brought them, and she had taken what she needed from the tides.

Still, in the quiet early mornings, when the village lay asleep and fog hung low over the hills, she sometimes thought of Pascal. He had been different from the others; kind in a way rare among men who lived by compass and cannon. She often recalled his stories, his words. When the wind carried a scent of salt and smoke, she let herself wonder, maybe it was Pascal whose kindness had left its mark in her womb.

Nevertheless, she was going to be a mother.

That was all she ever wanted. She refused to be denied again. A child woven from sea mist, warm spice and starlight. A child of her very own.

Colette could be found twirling with her long skirt through the streets of Rovona. The sun seemed to follow in her footsteps. She carried something timeless in her presence, as though she walked with the spirits of mothers past and the dreams of children yet to come. Children giggled as she passed, sensing the joy she held like a secret song. Elders nodded knowingly, eyes reflecting the quiet wisdom of generations. When she walked, her hand rested gently on her belly, a tender cradle for the life blooming within.

Beneath her smile, however, lay quiet trembling. She was further along now than ever before. Each day, joy walked hand in hand with fear. Still, she twirled. Because to move is to believe. To dance is to hope.

She covered herself in more clothing these days, more modestly, as if fabric could protect her unborn child. She no longer hid her orange curls beneath patterned scarves; her curls bounced freely on her shoulders as she walked proudly among the village streets.

"Bonjour," she said with a smile to everyone she passed. She brought flowers and laughter to her friend Margot, little treats for the baker, and bought coins and trinkets for her new hip scarf she was weaving, a testament to her flourishing creativity.

Her palm readings, once cautious, now spilled over with promise. Where once she saw trials and crossroads, she now saw blooming paths, open doors, fields ripe with possibility. The villagers noticed the change. Her pregnancy had become more than a private journey; she had become a vessel not only for new life but for new beginnings.

Once, not long ago, she had been the odd girl of the village; the barefoot dancer in the fields, the one who spoke to birds and knew the rain before it came. Whispers followed her for years of spells, strange dreams, and sorrow. Some feared her; most pitied her.

Now, people came to her.

Travelers with dust on their boots, families with woven baskets of offerings—dried herbs, coins, honeycomb. Children clutched their mothers' skirts, wide-eyed with wonder. They came for her good fortunes, to have their palms read beneath the sacred oak tree, to feel seen.

Her silly riddles continued but now brought rewarding predictions. Her mood was merry and captivating; men were drawn to her even more. Her new favorite riddle often spoken;

*Drunken fool*
*Drunken fool*
*Filled with lust and desire.*
*If you want good fortune with your crops*
*You must remember,*
*It is your WIFE that you desire…*

She would watch as the same men, to whom she spoke these words, held hands with their wives in town—honorable and gallant husbands. Colette felt a sense of accomplishment, as if she were quietly fixing broken homes, one husband at a time.

Tonight was the Harvest Moon Festival. The large orange moon would rise like a lantern above the hills, casting its spell over the village. This was her favorite time of year, the air turning crisp, the earth smelling of firewood and ripe fruit. Tonight was about abundance, about what had come to pass and what lay ahead, about letting go of fear and leaning into magic.

Autumn was beautiful.

Magic was strong this time of year. Colette could feel it humming in her bones. They said pregnancy brings a glow; with Colette, it was more than just a saying it was a presence. It radiated from her like orange mist at dawn, soft and otherworldly, wrapping around her as though the earth itself wanted to protect her.

Some said it was the child she carried. Others whispered it was the ancestors of the sea walking beside her, stirred by new life. And some said it was simply Colette herself, carrying the quiet strength of a woman who had suffered yet still dared to hope.

It was the magic of a body doing sacred work, the shimmer of creating life.

The villagers busied themselves hanging marigold and wheat. The scent of cinnamon and roasted chestnuts clung to the breeze. Filled with excitement for the evening, Colette took a long bath, humming a tune as she rubbed her belly, lavender soap lathering over her fingers and through her curls. Draped in rust-colored silks, her long skirt brushing the ground, she caught her reflection in a copper basin. For a moment, she saw what others saw, the Glow.

And for once, she allowed herself to believe it was real.

Not a trick of light, not flattery, but a fire lit within her by the life she carried and the love she refused to give up on.

Because some women are the lanterns,
And some women are the flame.

Chapter 35: The Palms and The Passing

In this line of work, Janell had learned to build walls without meaning too. At first, it was protection, a way to get through the shift, but over time, it became habit. When someone passed, the family was notified, the funeral home called, and soon after, the room was cleaned. A new resident would arrive with new medications, new family dynamics, and a fresh set of hopes and declines.

It was easy to become numb. Too easy.

She began to see it clinically, "actively dying," "comfort measures only," "DNR in place." The words softened the truth. She found herself answering families with practiced calmness, "It's a peaceful process," "she's not in pain," "we're keeping her comfortable." She believed it too—but sometimes it felt like reciting lines from a script.

As the social worker in this environment, Janell had a front-row seat to the last chapter of someone's life. Many had asked how she could work somewhere like this, a place where eventually everyone dies. But Janell knew death didn't diminish life. It defined it. It reminded her that time was precious and love mattered.

There was something holy about the last breath. Not necessarily religious, but in the quiet stillness of that final moment—when the room seemed to exhale with the body letting go—it felt sacred. Some residents passed peacefully, slipping away mid-sentence, mid-dream, mid-song. Others went slower, gasping, their bodies fighting what the spirit had already accepted.

Janell had seen families wail, collapse, scream. She'd seen others sit in stunned silence, not realizing until she whispered, "She's gone." Some needed to leave immediately; others stayed, watching the stillness settle over the person they knew. There was no training for this, no textbook to prepare her for the enormity of the moment. To witness someone's last breath was to be entrusted with something unspeakable.

She shouldn't have been in the room. Overdue psych consults, an upset daughter in the lobby, two new admissions she hadn't met yet. She hadn't eaten since breakfast or gone to the bathroom since seven that morning.

But something had pulled her here. Into a resident's room. Perhaps it was that the resident had been declining all week, and the nurse had mentioned she wasn't doing well. Janell took notice that no one was at her bedside.

She was dying. This resident, this woman.

Her breaths came like creaky door hinges, slow, laboring, borrowed. Janell wanted to feel something. But mostly she felt numb, dehydrated, hollow, as if her compassion had leaked out after the fifth family meeting that morning. The thought of another resident passing with no family present, another doctor scribbling "comfort measures only" and rushing off to lunch, was unsettling.

And then it happened.

Her resident took a breath so deep it didn't seem possible for a body so frail. The sound made Janell sit straighter.

Then—silence.

And that's when she saw it.

The air shimmered. Not metaphorically. Not poetically. Literally. A fine gold glimmer settled over the bed like morning dew. Her chest glowed from within—a soft, pulsing light, like a lantern deep inside a cavern.

Janell should have moved, called the nurse, logged the time. But her hand reached for the resident's hand instead, instinctively lacing her fingers into the frail palm. The skin was soft, faintly papery, and delicate as moth wings.

She traced slow, gentle circles with her thumb, right in the center of the palm.

It was something she had done dozens of times before, on the screaming, the scared, the slipping-away. It was strange how something so small could feel so powerful.

Her fingertip followed the lines and curves, and with each trace, her life unfolded—joys, regrets, stubbornness, grit. Janell saw that this woman had loved without apology and lived fiercely. The story of her rosed from her skin, not in words, not in images, but in feeling—the warmth still lingering beneath her skin.

A hum stirred beneath Janell's own skin, low and ancient.

She wasn't just stroking a dying woman's palm; she was opening a door, letting her pass, letting her know she was not alone. Suddenly, she wasn't a social worker in a dying woman's room. She was something else—a witness, a reader, a thread between worlds, a keeper of endings, a woman who remembered the ancient magic of touch.

And at that moment, there was no burnout.

No charts, no pressure, no paperwork.

Just the story of life.

She traced the soft skin a little longer as the resident exhaled one last time. Gentle. Light. As if she had been waiting for someone to truly see her before she left. Not clinically. Not diagnostically. But fully.

Her face softened in the quiet, and Janell lingered a moment longer.

Maybe for her. Maybe for herself.

Because for the first time in a long time, she felt it again; this work was sacred, and every day she got to do it was a gift.

## Chapter 36: Under the Stork's Gaze

The witching hour settled over the village like a dark, knowing breath.

The fire from the Harvest Moon Festival had burned low, the orange moon still cast a warm, golden hue over the fields and rooftops. Its surface, dappled with craters and shadows, seemed closer than usual, as if watching over the earth with a quiet, ancient presence.

The village slept, tucked in their warm beds, their dreams soft and full. But Colette was awake. At first, it was just a tightness in her belly, a strange, coiling ache that made her sit up in bed, one hand resting instinctively on her womb. She waited, breathing through it, thinking maybe the child had shifted, maybe it was just the restless stirrings of new life.

But then the pain increased.

It wasn't sharp, not at first. It was a deep, slow pull, like the tide retreating far too quickly. Like something being taken. She knew this feeling. She had known it before—twice.

She stood, holding the wooden bedpost with both hands, trying to steady herself as another wave hit, stronger now. Lower. Heavier.

"Please," she whispered—to no one. Or maybe to everything.

Her hand, slightly shaking, reached between her legs. The wetness she felt confirmed what she feared; the linens would be stained with blood, as they had been before. Her eyes began to water.

"Not again," she thought.

"NOT AGAIN!" she screamed into the darkness.
The walls seemed to tremble as she cried, a banshee wailing in the night.
Her heart pounded, her legs weak, the floor creaking beneath her. She fled her cottage into the night, down the pebble path, into the cool air, gasping for breath. Her nightdress billowed in the wind, soaked in sweat and something more tragic.

The dying fire from the festival still smoldered at the edges of the village square. Coals glowed faintly like forgotten stars, the remnants of celebration turned ash. Colette fell to her knees beside it, the impact jarring, the pain immediate. Her legs struck the embers, still hot, still alive. They bit into her skin, but she did not flinch.
She welcomed the sting.

And then she sobbed.

Uncontrollably. Her whole body heaved with the sound of a soul breaking open. Tears streamed down her face, soaking into the earth. Her fingers clawed in the soil as if she could pull her baby back from it. Around her, the embers pulsed like a fading heartbeat. The fire that had brought her joy, warmth, and dancing now bore witness to her collapse.

This child had come farther than the others.

Earlier, when the fire had roared and the music played, she had danced with this child under the harvest moon. Together, they were one. She had danced with her body, her spirit, her mind; every few moments, she pressed her hand to her belly. The entire evening had been magical, with conversations of her child to come.

To now, with this heart-wrenching pain flowing through her veins. The heat clawed at her legs, wrenching through her bones, a cruel reminder of the life she had lost. Smoke curled around her face, stinging her eyes, but she barely noticed. Each ember pressed against her skin like a question she could not answer, a punishment she did not deserve. Her chest burned with the fire of her own anguish, each sob wracking her body, leaving her gasping for air that would not come. The night was silent around her, yet every crackle and hiss of the dying fire felt like it echoed the torment inside her, relentless, and devouring.

Colette's tears poured without intention of stopping.

And then, she saw it.

Out of the haze of smoke and moonlight, standing at the edge of the square near the old well, there was a stork.
 The orange moon glowed behind it.

The bird stared at her, motionless.
 It stood with the solemn stillness of a statue.
 Colette blinked, unsure if she was dreaming or delirious. Its beady eyes did not blink. It stood absurd and elegant all at once, curious, perhaps mournful. Its presence was almost foolish in its simplicity, yet it radiated something deeper.
 A strange, quiet wisdom.

A witness.
 A strange, winged witness to her pain.

Through the tears, Colette's eyes met the bird's eyes as if the two of them were searching for each other's soul. Choked with tears, half-mad, between gasping breaths, she spoke,
 "Silly bird, why are you looking at me that way?"
 "Does my pain amuse you?"

The bird remained frozen, still glaring.

"Silly bird!" Colette yelled.

"With your long, skinny legs and your silly long beak. Go away!"

The bird stayed motionless, staring.

Her tone softened, "Silly bird, why does this keep happening to me? Please... can you tell me why? Why can't I be a mother?

"Was he right? Am I not meant to be a mother in this lifetime? Silly bird."

Wrapped in ash and sorrow, blood pouring from her legs and soaking deep into the earth, she knelt over the dying fire. Every heartbeat drove more crimson into the soil, her grief merging with the earth itself. Her chest heaved, sweat and tears streaking her face, and a hypnotic trance claimed her. She began to murmur at first, then the words tumbled out, raw and urgent, as if the earth itself demanded them.

*"Take three lives and replace them with three...*
*But know this,*
*in which lifetime could it be?*
*Grow three, but not from your family tree,*

*When this happens, you will clearly see...*"

Colette wiped her face; her cheeks were raw and tender.
She lifted her head to look into the stork's eyes once more.
She needed the stork at that moment.
She needed her silly, frozen friend.

But it was gone.
Her eyes searched though the thick trees and ominous woods.
It vanished silently into the orange glow of the night.
The stork had flown away.

Colette pressed her hand on her stomach, knowing the life that had been there was now gone. She felt empty.
In this haunting moment, with the warmth of the gravel and dirt pressing into her knees, the orange moon glowing above, her heart ached. Her insides pulsed with agony.
She had never felt more alone than at that very moment.
Colette stayed where she was, mumbling the same words repeatedly. Her body became frozen. Frozen like the stork.
Her gaze trapped in the light of the fire embers.

Her lips barely parted, again whispering,

*"Take three lives and replace them with three…*
*But know this,*
*in which lifetime could it be?*
*Grow three, but not from your family tree,*
*When this happens, you will clearly see…"*

And again, she whispered them once more.

## Chapter 37: Visions Beyond the Birth

Janell had two goals that day, make a sweet potato pie with her daughter and fold the gigantic pile of laundry waiting for her in the living room. Her daughter had been asking for weeks to make one. Of course, they would have to make two, her daughter and her husband loved sweet potato pie, and it always turned into a small war over the last piece. They had finally gotten all the ingredients at the grocery store the day before but had been too worn out from errands to bake.

Well—Janell had been worn out.

For weeks, she had been trying to move around as much as possible. Everyone kept telling her it looked like the baby was dropping. The pressure in her lower back was intense. Pillows and heating pads helped but never truly relieved the pain. Her kids have been amazing; making dinners, helping with chores, propping her feet up. They loved their mama and worried about her. The house had been full of penguin jokes as she waddled around lately.

She loved observing how pregnancy affected her kids differently—who was more cautious around her belly, who offered more help, who liked to feel the baby kick. It was fascinating to compare their personalities in such a process.

Her daughter eagerly got the ingredients out for baking day and preheated the oven for the sweet potatoes. Since they would be in the oven for at least 50 minutes, Janell told her to go play while she tackled the mountain of laundry. Instead, her daughter sat cross-legged on the ground next to her, offering to help. Sweet girl. They scrolled through Disney Plus together, trying to decide between *Ratatouille, Encanto,* or *The Little Mermaid.* If it were up to her daughter, she would probably turn on YouTube.

Janell leaned forward, tossing a folded towel onto a pile across from her.

And it happened.

The gush.

She told her daughter quickly to hand her back the towel and clumsily tried to get to her feet. The trickle continuing down her legs confirmed what she already knew.

Her water had broken.

There was no clear connection, but Janell couldn't help thinking about it; with her three biological children, contractions had always come first, and the medical staff had to break her water at the hospital. With this pregnancy, and the two surrogacy pregnancies before, her water had broken on its own before contractions began. Just a random thought as she stuffed the towel between her legs and waddled around gathering what she would need for the hospital. They were still two weeks away from the due date, but clearly, the baby was ready.

She told her daughter to turn off the oven.

"Wait, does that mean... no pies?"

The look of disappointment spread across her daughter's face as she realized their baking day had turned into a hospital day. Janell reassured her that the pies would get made in a couple of days and reminded her that the baby was ready to come. She told the kids to get in the car; their dad would leave work and meet them at the hospital. With a towel between her legs and several silly jokes about Mom peeing herself in the car, they made it to the hospital parking lot.

Janell was calm and confident—this was her sixth time doing this—but she still acted quickly. She knew from experience that the baby came faster with each pregnancy.

No time to dilly-dally. It was time to have a baby.

She got checked into the labor and delivery ward. Her husband met them, taking the kids to the hospital cafeteria to get them settled before returning to her. She started making calls to the surrogacy agency. The liaison got the message to the intended parents right away. They were in the United States, but states away and would be catching a flight as soon as possible.

By baby number six, Janell felt like a pro at checking in. They began triage; she disclosed her pregnancy history to the nurse and changed into a gown. Vital signs were taken, and the electronic fetal monitor was placed on her belly. The staff confirmed her water had broken, and a cervical exam showed she was already dilated to five centimeters.

Active labor.

She was admitted to a labor and delivery room. She told the nurse she was a surrogate and explained that the parents were on their way but would likely miss the birth. The nurse seemed curious about the surrogacy process and asked if Janell wanted to hold the baby and share a room with him before the parents arrived. Janell assured her she did. They discussed medication options.

Umm, yes and yes. She was okay with all the drugs, she joked.

Even though she was calm, Janell tried to find a tranquil place inside herself to lower her anxiety. No matter how much experience you had, childbirth was still childbirth.

The contractions began to make their appearance.

Fun. Fun. Not really.


She gripped the side of the hospital bed as another contraction rolled in, tightening around her belly like a powerful wave. She closed her eyes and breathed slowly in, slow out. Every few minutes the pressure returned, stronger, deeper, impossible to ignore. The space between each wave shortened. The nurse came in again, smiling as she checked her progress.

"Six centimeters. Your body's working beautifully."


The contractions became relentless, crashing over her like tidal waves with hardly any space between. Her body shook from the effort. Her jaw clenched.

Her husband announced the best news. "The anesthesiologist is here."


She hunched over, bracing for one more contraction. The needle felt small compared to everything else she was feeling.

Within moments, the edge softened.

The tightness remained, but the pain dulled, distant now.

About a half hour later, "You're nine centimeters," the nurse said, smiling.

Janell laid back, eyes closing a little, her body still surging with purpose.

With the epidural, the pain was manageable, but the pressure remained unmistakable.

The doctor on call entered with calm urgency, pulling on gloves and a blue gown as she spoke. She took her place between Janell's legs. A tray clinked with sterile instruments. The lower half of the bed dropped down, stirrups raised. The room became a stage for something powerful and raw.

"You're fully dilated," the nurse said excitedly.

"Time to push."

Her husband held her hand. "That's it. Big breath. Push just like that."

Janell bore down with everything she had. Rested. Pushed again.

The pressure was overwhelming, deep and heavy.

She could feel the baby moving down.

A deep roar came from somewhere inside her, ancient and strong.

"He's crowning," the doctor said. "Slow and steady now. Breathe through this, one more big push and he's out."

Janell groaned low and deep, a sound from her bones.

With a final roar, she gave everything she had.

And then—relief.

Wait. Everything went dark.

Complete darkness.

Something was not right.

A bolt of electricity shot through her. Her mind flashed with images, hurling through her brain so quickly the sensation was suffocating. When the whirlwind settled, she suddenly felt light and airy. She saw what appeared to be a city, busy streets and people roaming. She hovered over it all, as if watching a movie from above. A sign read Café du Dome.

Paris.

The atmosphere was lively, sometime in the 1920s by the look of it. One woman stood out, dancing on the cobblestone streets with musicians and street performers. She radiated joy. Her laughter harmonized with a violinist's melody. A man joined her, spinning her before diving into her arms. Their passion and love were unmistakable.

Then, another flash.

Janell's mind spun again, another hundred years back. On the horizon rose a circus tent, bold white-and-red stripes glowing. Everywhere, animals loading out of railcars, ropes pulled tents, curtains raised. Banners read Volcano Man, Queen of the Amazons, Tattooed Beauty. A poster off to the side caught her eye: PSYCHIC – Prophecies & Divinations Unveiled.

Behind it, a tent flap opened just enough for her to peer inside. A woman sat at a small round table, a crystal sphere before her. The enchantress was beautiful, her dark hair nearly reaching her waist, but her face was dispirited. Who was she? Janell tried to get closer but—

It happened again. The pull from inside her mind, as if memories were shuffled like a deck of cards. Lightning struck again, racing through her veins. Her vision blurred, then cleared another hundred years earlier.

Now she saw a woman kneeling beside a smoldering fire. The woman was covered in dirt and ash, her hair wild, glowing orange near the embers. She was sobbing uncontrollably, wearing a nightgown spattered with blood, gasping for air.

What's wrong with her? Janell wondered.

Suddenly the woman by the dying fire looked right at her. Their eyes connected. Janell couldn't break free.

Was she speaking to her? Her lips moved but Janell was too far to hear. In the other visions the women had not noticed her.

This one did.

Was she shouting? This woman with wild orange curls, and tears streaming down her face.

Janell glanced slightly left.

Feathers?
Was she a bird?

The next thing she knew, her husband was standing over her, asking if she was okay. She was back in the hospital room. She heard the baby crying as the staff cleaned him. She believed the crying had snapped her back.

What were those images? Who were those women? Why did she feel so connected to each one? Was she really a bird watching them? The questions fluttered through her.

Her husband said that once the baby was completely out, she had thrown herself back onto the bed, which he thought was pure exhaustion.

Forget the questions. Forget the visions—for now.

She needed to hold him.

Once they had cleaned him, they brought him to her.

He was perfect—ten fingers, ten toes, full head of black hair. Seven pounds, eight ounces. Healthy.

She knew this was their time. Once the parents arrived, he would join them in another room.

Her husband sensed she needed time alone and said he would return later.

The feeling of holding him was magical.

"We did it," Janell whispered into his ear, nuzzling her face close to his. She inhaled his intoxicating baby aroma. She closed her eyes, breathing him in deeply. Knowing this was her last baby, she never wanted to forget this scent, this moment.

As she raised her head from his, her heart began to race.
An orange glow beamed off him.

She blinked hard, worried the pain medication was playing tricks on her. But there was no mistaking it. The baby glimmered faintly with an orange hue. The same hue twinkled off her own skin. It spread up her arms as she held him. Her heart pounded with adrenaline.

A nurse walked in. Janell was terrified she would notice.

"Everything okay in here? He's beautiful," the nurse said calmly. Nothing in her behavior suggested she saw anything unusual.

The baby's little fingers wrapped around Janell's pinky, as if gripping her on purpose. Goosebumps rose on her arms, yet his touch calmed her.

She inhaled deeply, exhaled slowly.

When she opened her eyes, the orange glow was gone. The baby was no longer cloaked in light. She examined her hands and arms, nothing.

Mixed emotions flooded her as she watched the clock. The later it got, the closer their separation came. She felt happy it had been a safe delivery, that he was healthy. A sense of achievement rushed over her, but also a bittersweet peace knowing this was her last surrogacy journey.

Some time passed.

Word came that the intended parents were checking in and would be there shortly. Janell knew these were her last moments alone with him. She held him close and whispered into his ear the same two words she had whispered to the last two surro babies when they left her arms for the last time.

*"Find me."*

She wasn't sure why she had said it the first time, but with the second and now the third, she felt she had too.

The nurse took him from the room.

Janell was alone.

She knew it wouldn't be long before cheerful, grateful parents arrived, thanking her and wanting every detail of the last 24 hours.

She sat in the quiet stillness of the room, her heart already aching a little.

She thought of her visions again, now that he was no longer in her arms—those soul-stirring visions from different eras, different women, different settings.

But they all felt the same in some way.

How was that possible?

Chapter 38: Sight of Power

Janell felt good.

It had been a couple of weeks since the birth and completing her third and final surrogacy felt right. She felt balanced, truly balanced. Her thoughts wandered to her job. Being a social worker was never easy, but it allowed her to stand beside people in their final moments, to honor the last pages of their stories. And lately, through surrogacy, she had cradled a beginning as well—a first breath, a first cry. She felt stretched between endings and beginnings, holding both sides of life at once. Both roles revolved around transitions. As a surrogate, she was the vessel carrying life into the world. As a social worker in a nursing home, she was the one who gently guided life out. Both required intimate emotional labor without long-term attachment.

These roles carried weight, and the personal and professional lines often blurred. She was not the baby's mother, but she dreamed about him. She was not the resident's daughter, but she was there when they took their last breath.

Life, she realized, was such a strange and delicate balance.

The fog from the day she gave birth still lingered. Time felt warped, days slipping into one another as her body worked to heal.

The cryptic riddle that had once haunted her sleep no longer visited her dreams; instead, she drifted each night into vivid scenes from lives she barely remembered. Every morning, she woke with new fragments—glimpses of places, faces, and moments that felt both foreign and familiar. She savored piecing them together like a puzzle. Different stories, different loves, unfolding behind her closed eyes. What amused her most were the similarities—her mannerisms repeating across centuries, the kinds of people she gravitated toward, the souls she befriended again and again as if drawn by some invisible thread.

In every lifetime she saw new bodies and unfamiliar faces, but the same patterns kept resurfacing.

The puffiness of afterbirth had lessened. The cabbage had dried up her milk, just as with the surrogacies before. She needed to get out of the house, maybe even think about returning to work. Without bringing home a baby, she didn't technically need six full weeks of maternity leave; time for her body to heal, yes, but her mind perhaps even more so.

Many women feel an unexpected emptiness after giving birth, the body suddenly hollow, the baby no longer nestled inside. But for a surrogate, the sensation carries a different weight. You carried this child knowing you would place them into someone else's waiting arms. Your stomach feels strangely vacant; your hand still drifts there out of habit. But your body is slower to understand. Your breasts ache, your mind spirals, instinct clawing at you with the same primal confusion: *Where did the baby go?* Mother Nature becomes confused. She pulls at your spirit, your feelings, your emotions when you least expect it.

Janell closes her eyes and remembers that day in the hospital room, the way an orange glow shimmered across the walls, warm and strangely alive. She remembers holding him, his tiny weight settling into her arms as though he had always belonged there. The light had wrapped around them like a blessing, a quiet magic she still can't explain, as if the room itself understood the sacredness of their brief time together. Even now, she can feel it, that glowing hush, that moment suspended between meeting and goodbye. The magic of that day has never left her. It lingers in her memory, soft as breath and bright as the light that touched them both.


These restless, lingering feelings had pulled her here, perhaps that's why Janell now found herself perched on a barstool, menu in hand. She'd driven past this pub for years without a second glance, but today her car slipped into the parking lot as if it had made the choice for her. All she asked of herself was simple, a drink, and a hot meal to carry home.

Janell slipped onto a barstool, scanning the room quietly before ordering her comfort meal to-go and a glass of wine while she waited. "Pinot Noir please," she told the bartender. Then, almost as an afterthought, "And pie for dessert." Another bartender joined the one who had taken Janell's order. She was young as well, with the kind of striking features so many seemed to have these days—the classic Kardashian look. Regardless, she was stunning. It seemed this place only hired attractive staff. Janell noticed her hurry. She came in quickly, likely running late for her shift. Tossing a gym bag and an oversized water jug onto a bench behind the bar, she pulled her long dark hair into a swift ponytail. The water jug caught Janell's eye, plastered with stickers from top to bottom.

At the center, a sticker of a stork carried a baby in its beak.

She smiled at the serendipity of the moment. After all, she was only in this pub because her emotions were still raw from the birth, and somehow this small, whimsical image felt like a quiet acknowledgment of everything she had carried and given life to.

Janell caught herself envying the two bartenders—their youth, their effortless confidence—for a moment longer than she preferred.

Sure, she had the kangaroo-pouch belly. But who fucking cared?

That belly had carried six healthy pregnancies.

Her three children, and three more children for three deserving families.

She took a slow sip of her wine, letting her inner monologue steady her, feeding her truth just moments after admiring girls half her age. Six lives existed on this earth because of this belly—this so-called kangaroo apron or whatever insulting name women had come up with lately. Six humans who would grow, change, influence, and touch the world in ways she could only imagine.

This body had done that.

Six souls had been created and carried within this remarkable body of hers.

Her body was strong. Her body was resilient. Damn, was it resilient.

A woman's body was powerful.

And tonight, Janell felt powerful.

Wine in hand, she studied her reflection in the mirror behind the bar, tucking a stray hair back. Waiting on her to-go order, that was when a man slid onto the stool beside her.

"I like your tattoos," he said.

"Thanks."

He was attractive in a tired way. He had dark hair threaded with gray, blue slacks worn from the day, brown dress shoes, a bashful smile. But up close, his face bore the weary marks of a drinker, a smoker.

"This place gets busy on Friday nights after nine," he offered, searching for common ground.

"I won't be here that late," Janell replied. "I'll be in sweatpants, finishing dessert in bed by then."

Her directness seemed to catch him off guard.

The bartender returned, offering another round, but Janell shook her head. The man—Tony, as he later introduced himself—kept talking. Cars. Income. Prowess in bed. Salesman energy. A wedding ring glinted on his finger.

Janell glanced at the wedding ring on Tony's finger and gave him an exaggerated really? expression.

"Tony, you have a nice night. My to-go order should be ready soon," she said with polite finality, turning her barstool away to end the conversation.

Behind her she heard him grunt—dramatic, irritated.

"Okay," he muttered, "but you're missing out on the best night of your life."

He let out a low laugh that made her skin crawl. Then the scrape of his barstool, the uneven shift of his weight.

"You seem stuck-up anyway," he added, louder now, stupidity spilling through.

Normally Janell would de-escalate—smooth the edges, keep the peace, keep the world comfortable.

But not tonight.

Tonight, she wasn't interested in being pleasant. Or quiet. Or non-confrontational.

Especially not after he mumbled, "You don't even know me."

Janell turned slowly, slouching forward, wine glass in hand.

Her voice was calm. Controlled. Soft as a scalpel.

"I bet I can predict a few things," she said.

Tony leaned in immediately—hooked.

"I bet you were an athlete in high school," she began.

"Probably impressive, too. Small town, not much competition. You still hold onto those memories, don't you? Because that was the last time you felt truly… special."

Tony blinked, confused, caught in her gaze. Her eye contact had shifted—steady, unblinking, deliberate. A subtle trance he didn't know he'd fallen into.

Janell continued.

"You were young then. Full of potential. Full of life."

Her voice softened, almost sympathetic.

"And now? Even though you try—and you do try, don't you, Tony?—you keep disappointing the people who love you most."

Tony swallowed.

"Life hit you hard," Janell said. "Whiskey hit you harder."

She lifted her glass, letting the stem rest between her fingers.

"I'd predict you're on your second marriage. Couple of kids. You adore them, I'm sure. You say bold things like, 'I'd die for my kids.'"

She tilted her head.

"But would you live for them, Tony? Really live? Make real changes?"

A pause.

"You won't."

Tony's mouth opened, but nothing came out. "Your second wife—she's more manageable than the first, isn't she?" Janell added. "Less fire. Easier to control.

But you still think about wife number one. Every day if we're being honest."

Tony's face twitched.

"You'll think about her during marriage number three, too," she said.

Janell leaned back, letting her words settle.

"But none of those women are your true love."

Her eyes dropped meaningfully to the glass in his hand.

"No, she is."

"Whiskey."

Janell's voice lowered, velvet and venom.

"You love her. The sound of ice against the glass. The warmth. The numbness. You believe you deserve her after a hard day—you believe you deserve her every day."

She took a sip of her wine, running her tongue along the rim without looking away.

"You choose whiskey over everything. Over your wife's requests. Over dance recitals. Parent-teacher conferences. School plays."

A quiet breath.

"And God, the promises, Tony. So many broken promises."

She straightened her posture. Refined. Final.

"You'll keep choosing her," she said softly, "until she destroys you."

The spell broke.

Tony blinked rapidly, leaning back as though she'd physically shoved him.

"What are you," he stammered, "a fucking fortune teller?"

He tossed back the last of his drink, signaled for another, and muttered under his breath as he walked away.

Janell couldn't help the small smirk, the quiet laugh that slipped from her lips.

He'd gotten the hint.
He walked away.

Her to-go order still not ready, Janell started to head toward the restroom, but her legs went weak, she gripped the edge of the wooden table in the pub when she stood up from the bar stool. Her mind spinning. The pub's voices around her fading as the vision consumed her.

She was no longer herself—no longer a woman waiting on a to-go order in a crowded pub but the stork again. Her feathers shone silver in the moonlight, her long wings stretched wide, testing the air. The tang of salt clung to every breath, and she felt the rhythm of the sea crashing below.

She perched near the shore, silent, watching.

A blind child stumbled across the sand, arms outstretched, small feet uncertain. The sea beckoned. Fear trembled in the child's frame, but still, she waded forward, water climbing higher, swallowing her slight figure.

Her wings twitched, ready to take flight, but she felt she was not meant to interfere. She knew somehow that she was only there to witness.

The child disappeared beneath the waves.
Moments stretched into eternity.

Then—she emerged.

Crawling back to shore, soaked and shivering, her eyes opened. No longer clouded with blindness, they burned with a strange brilliance. The girl blinked, and for the first time she saw. Saw not just the world before her, but something more. Her gaze seemed to pierce through veils unseen. Janell's heart raced. She felt the heat of prophecy pressing against her ribs, as though the child's awakening sight were meant for her, too.

The pub returned in a sudden rush—the clatter of mugs and laughter shaking her back to reality. But Janell's hands still trembled.

Her vision loosened its grip, but the truth stayed burning inside her.

Putting the pieces together, Janell realized the seer of lifetimes past had been broken by the sea spirits, yet powerful enough to forge her agony into a prophecy of her own making.

The night the seer lost her third child; bleeding into the soil, her words were so powerful; that sorrow had rippled across centuries, waiting, waiting… until now.

And now—Janell understood.

The seer's suffering was not wasted; her pain had given rise to a destined future.

The sea spirits saw only a weak blind child wandering into the water. Tricksters, they believed they were taking the most powerful thing a woman carries—her womb.

The sea spirits thought they had forged a villain when they shattered her. But a woman who claims her power is no monster— she is a goddess.

They broke her, they tried to shape her into darkness, and yet here she stands, lifetimes later; unstoppable, fierce, and unbound.

The trick was on them.

Janell pressed a hand against her chest and let the thought bloom. I am not the blind child. I am not the one who was robbed of creation.

Janell was a woman who had brought forth life, not once, not twice, but six times. Six children placed on this earth, six flames she had kindled into being. Where the seer's womb had been taken, Janell's had overflowed.

The prophecy had not chained her to loss; it had sharpened her, forged her into something the sea spirits had never foreseen. For the first time, she realized she was not merely inheriting a prophecy.

She had fulfilled it.

Her mind drifted to Colette's powerful words that night, a prophecy of her own making. She had seen it unfold through the stork's frozen gaze.

*Take three lives and replace them with three…*
*But know this,*
*in which lifetime could it be?*
*Grow three, but not from your family tree,*
*When this happens, you will clearly see…*

"I *see* my power," she whispered.

Her to-go order sat ready, but Janell's eyes were locked on the mirror behind the bar. What stared back was no mere reflection. Her irises burned molten orange, fire spilling from within, illuminating the truth of herself. Heat surged through her veins. Ecstasy and clarity collided, a deep knowledge that came from lifetimes she had carried, lives she had nurtured, and power that had always been hers.

The mirror cracked, jagged lines slicing through the glass with a sound that cut across the pub—part warning, part celebration. Patrons gasped; glass rattled.

Janell paid her bill, unfazed by the commotion. As she reached the door, she noticed Tony watching her.

"You never told me your name!" he called.

She paused, weighing her options, then glanced back over her shoulder.

"It's Colette."

*At last, her power had awakened*
*and as for her six creations,*
*They remained blissfully unaware of the reckoning she had begun.*

www.ingramcontent.com/pod-product-compliance
Lightning Source LLC
Chambersburg PA
CBHW031938240626
47153CB00003B/774